Best

is…Christmas wedding bells will be ringing if the Matchmakin' Posse of Mule Hollow can get this stubborn cowboy and cowgirl together under the mistletoe for the most anticipated kiss of the holiday.

Will Ty Calder, mild mannered partner in the New Horizon Ranch, get his secret Christmas wish and heal his lonesome heart this season? Find out in Book 4 of the New Horizon Ranch/Mule Hollow series.

Horse trainer Ty Calder did the right thing four years ago and sent his best friend, Mia Shaw off with a hug and best wishes in her quest for her rodeo dreams to come true. But now she's back for the Christmas holiday and he's not sure he can send her off again without revealing his true feelings…

Mia is back in Mule Hollow healing up from an injury that could end her run for the championship. But, lately her heart's not been completely committed to her rodeo dreams and Ty has her thinking he might just be the reason.

Suddenly, tensions are running high between Mia and Ty…sparks are flying and have been spotted by the Matchmakin' Posse. Now these two are dodging mistletoe, matchmakers and the kiss they're both fighting to avoid and longing for.

But Ty can't believe Mia is ready to give up on her dreams when she's so close…he knows it means more to her than most people realize. No matter how much he wants a life with Mia he refuses to stand in the way of her dreams even if it means losing her forever…

It may take his four partners at the New Horizon Ranch and the town of Mule Hollow to get these two believing Christmas is especially the time that love can conquer all.

This is going to be one Christmas these two will remember forever…

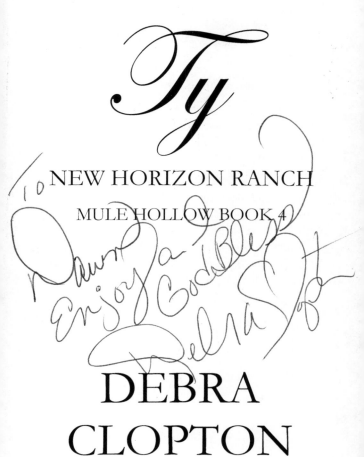

Ty

NEW HORIZON RANCH

MULE HOLLOW BOOK 4

DEBRA
CLOPTON

TY

ABOUT DEBRA CLOPTON

Bestselling author Debra Clopton has sold over 2.5 million books. Her book OPERATION: MARRIED BY CHRISTMAS has been optioned for an ABC Family Movie. Debra is known for her contemporary, western romances, Texas cowboys and feisty heroines. Sweet romance and humor are always intertwined to make readers smile. A sixth generation Texan she lives with her husband on a ranch deep in the heart of Texas. She loves being contacted by readers.

Visit Debra's Website and sign up for her newsletter for news and a chance to win prizes
http://debraclopton.com

CONTENTS

CHAPTER ONE

Ty Calder was lonesome.

Christmas was almost here and for all of his adult life Ty's Christmas wish had been for the opportunity of a do-over…but he'd lived long enough to know that Christmas wishes very seldom came true. Christmas wishes were for children after all.

Pushing his restless thoughts aside he strode into the county auction barn to check on the two colts he had in the sale today. Two weeks till Christmas and there was a threat of snow in the air. If the weather kept this up Mule Hollow, Texas might get a white Christmas this year.

Several cattlemen standing around a gas heater in the corner greeted him and he paused to shake the hands of Applegate Thornton and Stanley Orr.

The two older men couldn't hear worth anything but they had great eyes for a good horse or a good heifer.

"You two looking to buy," he asked, taking the moment to warm his hands, rubbing them together in the heat.

"Naw," Applegate boomed as the perpetual frown on his thin wrinkled face lifted slightly at the corners, for him this was a big smile. "We're here to enjoy the show."

"Ha!" Stanley grinned causing his rounded cheeks to lift high as his booming reply caused nearby cattle to jump. "We like to watch you younger cowboys pick livestock. *You* know yor horses, but thar are some who ain't quite got yor eye. If you know what I'm talkin' about."

"It can be plum entertaining to watch," App added with a smirk.

Ty chuckled. "You two find your entertainment in odd places—" A sudden shout had him spinning to see a woman with a brace on her knee struggling with a horse in the parking lot. The horse reared and the woman stumbled back.

Ty charged forward to help.

The woman managed to stay on her feet, though the leg with the brace looked stiff as she moved back from the gelding that was in the midst of a full blown fit. If someone didn't get him under control the woman wouldn't stand a chance. Especially with that obvious problem with her leg.

Ty reached her while the horse pawed the air. He grabbed the reins in a firm grasp, kept his eyes locked on the horse and fought for control. "Whoa there," he crooned.

"What are you doing?" the woman demanded, refusing to let go.

The big gelding smashed its front feet to the ground and yanked on the reins. Its eyes were wild and its ears were flattened to its head—not a good sign.

"I'm getting this horse under control." Ty shot the stubborn woman a glance and almost let go of the reins-Mia Shaw glared back at him.

Mia.

"I can do it myself," she snapped, her grip hardening beneath his. The horse jerked in response to the added tension.

If the horse had kicked Ty in the gut it wouldn't have knocked the wind out of him like seeing Mia had just done.

He couldn't believe his eyes. Seeing her, he suddenly felt as tongue-tied as he'd once been in school. Mia had sat in front of him in English class and he'd been a blundering idiot at that time.

If he'd tried to speak to her, his words twisted inside and wouldn't come out. It was as if he couldn't say anything right around her. Even if he got words out they were basically a jumble of just plain embarrassing mumbo jumbo.

What had been wrong with him?

Mia had made his world spin, that's what. Just looking at her and being near her had been torture because he was so tied up in knots around her.

And then, one day out of the blue, she'd asked him to help her learn to ride.

Riding was his comfort zone. He could talk about horses and could ride anything. And thus he'd pushed his crush to the back burner and became her teacher. And also her friend. As her friend he could talk to her.

Once their friendship had become solidified, taking the chance to try and become more had been impossible. By then, he'd learned and saw what her dreams were…and they didn't include living in this small town and marrying a cowboy. This cowgirl had her eyes on rodeo glory just like her late father once had…she'd lost so much in her life that there was no way Ty was going to try and get in the way of her dreams coming true.

But his world had always begun and ended with thoughts of her. He'd always wanted the best for her. He was always praying she was having a good day and that this would be her year to win her championship.

No one had ever affected him like Mia Shaw.

And here she was standing in front of him, eyes as blue as a bluebird and hair as silky and golden as a palomino. For him, no one had ever come close to Mia…

The horse jerked and let out a snort that brought Ty to earth once more.

If he didn't do something about this horse, he

and Mia both were about to get kicked to the ends of the earth and he would never get the opportunity for that do-over he'd been praying for.

"Let go, Mia," he said calmly and was forever grateful that he'd managed to come up with those words.

"I can do it. *You* let go. It's my horse."

Was she kidding?

"No, Mia. Let go."

The horse jerked again. "Whoa," Ty urged, managing to sound calm when, in fact, his blood pressure skyrocketed. Feeling her hand beneath his, feeling the firmness in her grip, and the determination in her eyes all told him she wasn't giving in.

Well if she wasn't letting go, he certainly wasn't.

They'd do this together.

She glared at him. "I can do it," she gritted through clenched teeth.

"Not on my watch," he growled. "If you're going to hang on, then, baby, I'm going to hang on too."

The horse pulled back, pawing at the earth.

"Come on, boy, calm down," Ty urged, as the horse reared again, its hooves flailing madly in the air. Ty grasped Mia's arm with his free hand and yanked her out of the way as he moved between her and the horse. He ignored Mia's disgusted mumbles as he shortened the rope and held firm. Determined to wrangle this piece of irritating horse flesh into his control Ty dug his boot heels into the ground and drew the reins even shorter. His arm strained with the effort of physically holding the horse to the ground. The animal swung its body attempting to take him and Mia out that way. They moved quickly to stay out from under it but Mia stumbled sideways and molded herself to Ty's side, her soft curves taking his attention off the horse. Their gazes locked momentarily before she pushed away.

The horse jerked powerfully on the rope forcing Ty to refocus.

Mia could never, ever have held on to this horse.

Ty managed it only because this was what he did. He took wild, unbroken horses and trained them. But not this horse…he'd realized during the struggle that he knew this horse.

He could feel Mia's fury beside him but at the moment he didn't care. She would have been hurt and he knew that now because this horse was crazy.

He held firm and through force of will led the horse over to the trailer where he tied it securely to the side bar then he spun toward Mia. She'd finally let go of the animal and stood waiting on him with an expression as angry as he felt.

At least she was standing out of the danger zone.

"What were you thinking? That horse would have kicked you. It would have stomped you. You had no control—"

"I had control of the horse—" she snapped, thrusting her shoulders back as she stepped toward him.

"You had no control of that horse. None." He couldn't believe after all these years, *all these years* of wanting to speak to Mia that here he stood and he was furious and almost shouting at her.

This was not the way he'd dreamt that they might one day meet again. Nope, he'd dreamed they'd meet and he'd prove to her that he wasn't a blooming idiot who couldn't talk to the woman he was awe-struck over.

The woman who was, at the moment, red faced with anger. "I…that is my horse," she stammered. "And I know what I'm doing."

"I couldn't tell that you did. If you'd have known what you were doing you'd have let me have control of that horse instead of taking your life into your hands and risking getting stomped. Especially when you knew I had him."

She huffed, "I did not know such a thing. The horse just reared up. I was going to get him under control. I was."

Ty ground his molars to keep from saying anything more. Fumes were surely billowing out of his ears–he could feel them. Hot as fire and crackling as he fought not to say something else that would cause this to go any further in the wrong direction. "I can see," he managed tightly, carefully. "That you might have thought that you

9

knew what you were doing. But how in the name of thunder…" he said, tighter as his temper started creeping up again, "…did you load that horse?"

He'd recognized the horse finally after getting over the shock of seeing Mia again. He knew where she'd gotten it. It was one that her uncle, who lived about fifteen miles outside of town had bought at an auction one day when Ty was there.

Not that her uncle ever spoke to him, but he did see him on occasion and as Stanley would say, her uncle, Huey Shaw, despite being one of the older men in town, had no eye whatsoever for good horseflesh.

And he was right. This beast was about as worthless as they came.

And of course *her* uncle had bought it and taken it home and now because of this horse Mia was in danger of her life! It should have gone to someone who *at least* had a little understanding of what a horse needed in order to be tamed. Or at least controlled.

Mia's eyes flashed fire. "I was able to load it," she said, enunciating each word. "And I would have been able to get it into the auction barn."

"You don't know what to do with him. So you brought him back to the auction to resell. Isn't that right?"

Her head cocked to the side and those amazing eyes of hers narrowed and he got distracted looking down at her. Boy she looked hot... Really hot. Hot as in really good to look at, she was beautiful and he couldn't believe he was standing here with her again. But she looked about as hot as a chili pepper, too and it dawned on him that give her a little bit more ammunition and she might haul off and crack him across the jaw.

Not that she'd ever been the violent type, but of course for some reason right now she was fumingokay, it could be the fact that she had in her own mind *thought* she could control this animal.

Ha! It just went to prove that she was really, really kin to her uncle.

"Okay, you are absolutely correct," he managed, getting control of his own temper at long last.

She looked a little contrite at his agreement.

"Well, maybe I couldn't have gotten control of him. But he's my horse and I don't need you tending to my business."

It was so ridiculous he chuckled—"I wasn't tending to your business. I was saving your hide." Maybe he shouldn't have said that, or chuckled. Maybe, just maybe, he should have kept his big mouth shut. But um, it was a little too late for that.

So much for the dream…nope, she would probably never speak to him again now that he'd finally gotten his shot—gotten his do-over.

And what had he done?

Opened his big mouth and inserted…no, he'd *stuffed* his big, booted foot into it…

CHAPTER TWO

"Saving my hide?" Mia snapped, wanting to disappear. She hated to admit she was in over her head with this horse but with her bum knee, she was. The maniac horse had given her nothing but trouble all morning but she'd managed to stay alive. Then the ornery beast just had to completely freak out here at the auction barn.

And then, Ty showed up and witnessed it all.

Anyone else would have been fine. But not Ty Calder.

"So are you trying to sell him?"

"My uncle wants to sell him." Needed to sell him was more accurate but Ty didn't need to know that.

Ty's brows scrunched cutely beneath his cowboy hat as he pinned his dove gray eyes on her.

She'd always found him so handsome and the cowboy had only gotten better with age.

"Acting crazed like he is that horse isn't going to bring much if anything."

"Why do you say that?"

"Because no one in their right mind is going to put good money on a lunatic horse. He's unreliable and dangerous. You know that, Mia. There isn't any guarantee his temperament will change."

She groaned inwardly. "He's from a great bloodline and that counts," she argued weakly, knowing full well what he said was true though she'd had to take a chance coming to the auction.

"It's got *great* bloodlines. But unless he's polished up, at least a little, no one in their right mind is going to touch him. Not for the price your uncle paid for him."

Her uncle had absolutely no horse sense. And worse, not really any ranching sense. He'd come into ranching by default when he'd come to her rescue the day her parents had been killed in a car wreck. She'd been twelve, heartbroken and lost. He'd come to her rescue, left behind his life in

Waco and stepped into a world he knew nothing about so she could remain in her home where she'd lived with her parents.

"Wait. How do you know what he gave for him? Were you there?"

"I was."

She grimaced. "He bought Sinbad for me to compete with. He refused to tell me how much he paid but he thought this horse..." she waved a hand toward the willful horse, "...would be the one to give me a real shot at the championships."

It was his turn to grimace. Ty knew horses and she knew that he knew this was impossible. Given the fact that the horse was crazy and needed major training before there could even begin to be a chance that it could be used to compete for the national titles that she was competing for. And time.

"That explains it," Ty said, almost apologetically. "I had thought about bidding myself but they started the bids way out of the ballpark."

This time she groaned out loud. "You know Uncle Huey, he tried so hard to take to ranching

15

but he was terrible at it. But he wanted me to go after my dreams and he tried…" she let her words trail off thinking about those dreams.

"We all wanted you to go for your dreams and you're doing great. But him thinking this horse could help was a really bad idea. And trying to sell him like this isn't a good one either, Mia. Sinbad's reputation preceded him and everyone knew he was a time-bomb. *Is* still," he amended, shooting the horse a glance.

Great. Just great. The weight on Mia's shoulders grew heavier.

"Mia, my heart is still thundering from thinking about you nearly getting trampled by this horse. Why are you the one here doing this? And with a bum leg?"

Mia stared at him. "I'm doing it because when I arrived home last night I found Uncle Huey trying to get Sinbad into a stall and it's a wonder he didn't get himself killed. When I asked him what he was doing he told me he was selling him. And so I loaded Sinbad up this morning and headed for the auction."

"And you nearly got yourself killed."

Her eyes narrowed. "Ty Calder you know good and well that I can handle a horse. I'm not a novice."

"Under normal circumstances yes. This horse isn't normal." His forehead wrinkled over skeptical eyes. "How did you get it loaded?"

Her jaw dropped at the insult. "I am not going to acknowledge you even asked me that."

He had the decency to look a bit embarrassed. "Look, I know you can handle a normal horse. This one's not normal."

This was going nowhere but downhill. "You know what, forget it. I've got business to take care of." She started to walk off and he grabbed her arm.

"Wait a minute. I didn't mean to insult you. What if I take him back with me for a few days and work with him? I might even buy him—"

"No, I don't need you buying a horse you clearly think is a junk."

"Hey, remember I was going to bid on Sinbad before they jacked the starting bid up and Huey

17

jumped into the ring. Give me two weeks with him to settle him down at least. It'll be a good challenge for me. Then you give me first dibs on him before taking him to auction."

She studied him. "Is there an auction the week of Christmas?"

"A big one."

She wanted to tell him no. But, she knew when it came to training a horse Ty was one of the best. And she did have a bum knee. And Ty had a gift and if she really wanted to help her uncle and get top dollar for Sinbad then the only thing she could say was yes. "You're sure you have time?"

"I'll make time for you and your uncle."

Her stomach knotted. So much for her plans to avoid Ty while she was home. "If you're sure then I'll say yes for Uncle Huey."

A flicker of a smile crossed his lips. After a second he nodded. "Then, let's load him up and take him to my ranch."

This was not how she'd expected the morning to go. This entire trip home was not like she'd expected so far.

Ty knew there was no way even he could get this horse into shape in two weeks. But he was confident enough in his abilities to know he could help at least teach it to be manageable. Which translated into safer for Mia and in better shape than it was now.

All the way back to the ranch Ty tried to wrap his mind around the reality that Mia was here. She was injured, and though they hadn't had time to get into that, he was curious about why she was wearing that brace and how long she wasn't going to be competing.

His life had changed since Mia had gone away and he'd kept his feelings for her locked away. He'd distanced himself from her more and more as time passed by using work as an excuse. He'd had to do it because every time he'd talked to her over the phone, he'd had to fight himself not to expose his feelings for her.

But lately she'd been on his mind constantly.

Pulling into the ranch entrance he tried to focus

on one step at a time, getting the horse settled in a stall was first. Mia maneuvered her truck around and backed the long trailer in where he indicated. He watched her ease out of the truck and his heart clutched at the pain that briefly flashed over her face.

"I've got this," he said going to the back of the trailer where he carefully unloaded the temperamental horse. It took a few minutes but he got it in a stall and felt a little relief that Mia hadn't tried to get in his way.

"So, now what?" she asked once they were both standing outside the sturdy stall gate with Sinbad eyeing them from behind it.

"Now, we give him the rest of the day to acclimate to this environment. I'll start working with him tomorrow. You're welcome to come out and watch. Or help some. But I'll need control."

"I'll be here. And I've already agreed to give you control for this two weeks." She looked around the stable. "Nice."

Nice was an understatement.

"Yeah, CC wasted no expense on his ranch."

"My uncle told me that you were one of five ranch hands to inherit the New Horizon Ranch from your boss."

"Yeah, CC shocked me and my partners when he left us his ranch. This beautiful place was his pride and joy." The reality of this enormous gift still hadn't completely registered in Ty's mind. "CC hand-picked us to carry on his dream and to live our dreams here on the ranch."

CC had died of cancer and he'd given up his law practice not long after realizing he was more than likely going to lose his battle with the offensive disease and he'd come to live at the ranch full-time. He'd put a lot of faith into Ty, Maddie Rose, Rafe Masterson Chase Hartley and Dalton Borne. Ty was over the horse program on the ranch and took his position extremely seriously. He'd forever be grateful to CC. As would his partners.

"I'm sure you'll do him proud. You've always been the best that I've ever known with a horse. CC must have recognized that."

"I like to think so." He didn't mention the

21

pressure he felt on his shoulders to build the program into one of the best in the state of Texas.

He and Mia walked out into the sunshine, her limping slightly.

"I need to go tell Uncle Huey about the change in plans. I'll come tomorrow," she said.

"You don't have to run off."

She was moving toward her truck and didn't pause. "I'm not. I just feel like I need to get back to the ranch and let Uncle Huey know what's going on."

"Mia," he said as she got into the truck and he could tell by the nearly hidden grimace when she got in that her leg was hurting. He placed a hand on the door. "What happened with your leg?"

She looked away and started the engine then looked across her shoulder at him. "Dog-gone ground doesn't always give when I jump off my horse and run after a goat. I'll see you tomorrow."

"Yeah, sure." Ty stepped back and closed the door then watched her pull away. The chill of the day had seemed to warm when she was around but now it seeped into him and as she disappeared out of sight he had the overwhelming urge to jump in his truck and race after her.

Tension, tightened like a steal band in his chest. Watching her leave wasn't something he could do again and he restrained from chasing her down only because he knew she'd return tomorrow. He had two weeks that he knew of and with her injury maybe he had a little more time. But right now two weeks was better than nothing.

CHAPTER THREE

Mia made it back to her uncle's ranch with her mind churning with thoughts of Ty. She'd known she would see him when she came home but she hadn't expected it to be so soon. Truth was, she'd been putting it off for four years.

And if she hadn't been so road weary...and lonesome over the last few months she might have stayed away longer. But her injury and the feeling in her gut that her uncle needed her had made it impossible not to come home to Mule Hollow for the holidays.

Once the desire to be a champion was all she'd lived for. But...she couldn't say her heart was in it so deeply these last months.

Her uncle was coming out of the barn when she pulled into the yard. He'd looked so stressed last night and again today. In his late sixties, he was average height with a comfortable pudge around his middle and thinning hair that was a mixture of gray and dark brown. He was a loner with a gruffness to him that had always intimidated her when he'd first come to live with her. She'd long since decided that the gruff exterior was a cover-up for shyness. Today he just looked distracted and stressed. More guilt piled onto her shoulders. She should have come home sooner.

"Uncle Huey, are you feeling poorly?" She was certain now that something wasn't right. He was withdrawn and though he'd always been quiet this was different.

He halted with his hand on the railing of the steps to the porch. "I just have things on my mind. How did it go at the sale?"

She hesitated, then told him what had happened. He didn't even look like he was paying full attention to what she said. Instead, he kept looking toward the door as if he wanted to go inside.

"Hon," he said, calling her what he had called

her for years. "Do what you want with the horse. The money from it will be yours anyway." He hurried up the porch steps to the house.

Mia didn't like the sound of this. Was her uncle depressed? She limped after him. "Uncle Huey, are you okay? Seriously. You seem so unhappy. Can I help? I promise we'll get as much money for Sinbad as possible."

He stopped on the porch, which needed some boards nailed down tighter and could use a new coat of paint. It struck her again that she had no idea what his financial situation was but from the look of things money was tight. All the more reason buying Sinbad for her as a gift made no sense. Mia had been winning enough to keep her dream alive on her own dime. The minute she couldn't keep sponsors to help keep her afloat or win enough to pay her entry fees and gas and food then she'd always said she'd get a real job. But, though she wasn't rolling in the dough, she was paying her own way.

But she wasn't helping Uncle Huey out with upkeep on the ranch. Should she have been?

"Uncle Huey," she said again, questioning as he was slow to answer her.

"Everything is fine, Mia. Stop worrying. I'm just…" he looked sad momentarily then frowned. "Nothing. I'm just restless."

Restless…Mia understood that feeling since she'd been feeling restless for months. She let him go inside this time without badgering him. But no matter what her uncle said, something was wrong. But what?

After Mia had left, Ty saddled up his ranch horse and rode out to the west pasture where they were doing a branding. As he loped across the pasture with thoughts of Mia and himself fighting for position over each other, he couldn't help smiling at all the good times they'd had riding and roping together. She'd been a natural and had soaked up riding like a sponge. She'd had a right to get mad at him this afternoon when he'd insulted her horse abilities. But with a brace and a reckless horse he was justified in his worry and he was standing by that.

"Hey, how did it go with the two colts?" Rafe Masterson asked as he rode up from where they'd gathered the cattle in the valley.

"Went good. They brought a good price." Since he'd left before the sale started he'd had to call the auction barn to find out what his colts had sold for.

Chase Hartley studied him, his gaze narrowing. "What's up? You look like you've got something on your mind."

Was it that evident? "An old friend was there who I haven't seen in a while. I brought her horse home to the ranch to work with it a little. She nearly got herself hurt."

Dalton one of his other partners looked up from where he was tagging a calf. "You sure you didn't bring it home because the owner might be pretty? I hear a little somethin' in your tone I'm not used to."

Maddie their female partner, who seemed to bring balance to the group of men, was standing beside the calf. She stuffed her hands to her hips and studied him. "I detect something too. I hope I'm right."

"Y'all, it's been a lot of years since I've seen Mia. We used to be really good friends. But we're just friends. Her Uncle Huey Shaw, y'all know him, he bought this rank horse and it's pretty loco. I'm just going to give it a few manners so she can get her uncle at least what he paid for the overpriced gelding. If it acts like it could turn into a decent horse I'll buy him for the ranch."

Maddie was grinning. "Wow. That's more than I've heard you say in most entire weeks. What's up with this?"

She wasn't the only one grinning from ear to ear—Chase, Rafe, and Dalton were all staring at him with grins.

Dalton laughed. "I think you might have been rambling," He stood up and let the calf free.

"That's what it sounded like to me," Rafe agreed.

Chase's gaze dug deep. "Do you like this gal?"

"Now y'all," Ty warned, not comfortable at all with their scrutiny. "Just hold on. I came out here to work. Not have the four of you to be gettin' ideas. Or anyone else for that matter."

All of them were fairly new to being married and despite that being part of what had made him start having a harder time of ignoring the longing for Mia in his life, he didn't want them getting into his business. He'd handle this in his own time. Having brought Sinbad here might have been a wrong move on his part. Maybe he should have said he'd come to Mia's place and do the training. That was still a possibility.

"Alright already," Rafe chuckled. "Don't get all hot around the collar. Let's finish up here everyone so we can be on time for supper."

"Now that's the most logical thing I've heard since I rode up here," Ty said and headed off to do his part in rounding up the cattle for inspection and tagging.

But as he rode off his thoughts stayed on Mia and the situation he was now in.

Truth was, he was no lady's man. He was rough around the edges and short on words normally. So how was he supposed to not make a complete mess of wooing her?

Wooing…had he really just used that term?

He was in big trouble. He was in way over his head.

Mia tossed and turned that night as she slept. Her dreams were a mixture of confusion as her dreams intertwined with reality…she fought deep sleep, struggling not to give into the pull of the dreams of Ty. But she lost and found herself lost in the dream of arriving home for the first time and seeing Ty again after being away for so long…only this dream was a lot different than what had happened today…

…her nerves rattled and her heart pounded as she pulled her truck to a halt. Ahead of her in the arena was Ty. He was working with a beautiful colt, but it was Ty that her eyes locked on. Butterflies erupted in the pit of her stomach as she exited the truck, heart racing.

Ty turned toward her and her pulse exploded when his dove gray eyes met hers. She'd always loved his serious, thoughtful eyes. She lifted her hand in a small wave and laughed as shock registered on his handsome, dear face. This was what she wanted.

"Mia," he called in disbelief. He dropped the lead rope and strode toward the fence. He didn't bother walking down to the gate, instead, he climbed to the top of the metal arena and then hopped from the top to the dusty earth. He was so agile as he moved toward her with purpose in each stride. He wore a soft black tee-shirt that showed his firm chest and lean waist, and strong arms honed from continuously working with horses. His chaps hung low on his hips and as he moved her way the fringe danced happily with each step.

She started toward him, biting her lip as she went…when they were five feet apart she would have catapulted herself into his arms but held back. Even in sleep she understood the turmoil holding her back from exposing her feelings. He pulled her into the security of his arms.

"You're home," he said, his voice gruff against her ear.

A shiver of awareness moved through Mia and she sighed. Home. Yes.

Ty held her like that for a long moment and Mia could hardly breathe as she savored the feel of him. The lonesome, longing she'd had for this nearly undid her. Her arms went around him and for the briefest of moments she let herself *imagine that this was the hug of a man who loved a woman.*

It was bliss—

Mia woke at that. Even her subconscious understood self-preservation–thank goodness.

Wide awake and thankful to see the faint pink of daylight peeking through her curtains Mia got out of bed and dressed. She intentionally pushed away thoughts of the dream. But it lay there in her heart–a constant reminder of what she hoped for. Of what she feared she could never have. There was no way she'd expose her desire to take their relationship into the realm of romance...of love. For one, Ty had distanced himself from her over the last few years while she was away and she'd been angry at him. She'd say she'd been hurt but she hated how that made her feel weak...to allow a man to hurt her was unthinkable. She'd tried to keep her heart closed off from the pain of letting anyone get close to her. Her heart had locked up on her when she'd lost her parents.

But lately, these dreams and longing for Ty had been driving her to distraction.

She glanced into the office and Uncle Huey

looked up from his computer. "Good morning," he said, sounding a lot livelier than he had the last two days.

"Good morning to you. You're looking chipper this morning."

He grinned and her heart surged with love for the man who'd stepped in when she'd most needed someone. He'd given up his life in Waco to come take care of her and she'd never heard him complain at all.

"I'm sorry, I've been a little distracted. But today's going to be a great day."

She laughed, delighted by his enthusiasm. "Is something happening I should know about?"

His eyes twinkled. "It's a surprise. Later today."

"Okay," she said and had to struggle to hold her curiosity back. He was happy and she didn't want to push too hard. "I'm heading over to see Sinbad. Should I be back at any certain time today?"

"Will you be back by mid-afternoon?"

"Sure. Any time you need me."

He looked totally mischievous. "That'll be

alright."

She nodded. "Alrighty then, I'll see you around two or so."

What was her uncle up to? Mia tried to come up with what his surprise could be but she was at a complete loss as she slowed at the entrance of the New Horizon Ranch. Thoughts of the dream took over at that point. This, she reminded herself this was *not* her dream. Several trucks of cowboys pulling trailers behind them tuned onto the blacktop and headed down the road. Dust still lingered on the drive as she drove past the gorgeous Austin-stone home on the right and then across the large rock parking area between all the barns, arenas and stables. This was a large operation and unlike her uncle's place there was plenty of money to maintain the property and buildings. Ty was really all she had eyes for though. She spotted him instantly, drawn to him as he stood in the center of the arena. Just like in her dream…

Butterflies went wild in her stomach and intense heat burned her cheeks as she got out of the truck, wincing at the pain that shot through her knee.

She felt almost surreal and for a brief moment, she wondered if she'd really dreamed last night's dream...

"Hey," he called and started her way.

He looked as good as he had in her dream moving toward her. Ty climbed the fence and she knew this had been in her dream because it was a familiar move she'd watched him make all during the time she'd known him. The man was quick, lean and agile and to him fences were only meant to walk through if he just happened to be standing beside one when he needed to exit or enter an arena.

He dropped to the ground and strode toward her. The chaps were long and the fringe short and didn't wave as much as in her dream, but the intensity of his gaze and stride was similar. Her breath caught in her throat and she almost believed he might take her into his arms—but he didn't.

Nope, he stopped a few feet from her and tapped the coiled rope in his hand against his right thigh, looking every inch the cowboy that he was.

"You got here just in time," he said, warmth flickering in his gaze. "How's your knee?" He glanced down at her knee and the brace she wore over her jeans.

"It's fine."

"I wanted to ask you more about it yesterday but you ran off. Does it hurt bad?"

She didn't want to talk about her injury but at least it directed her thoughts from where they'd been. "If I'm careful it's fine. It's just a partial tear to my MCL. A bad twerk is all. If I move too suddenly it hurts like the dickens though. The doctor says it just needs some time."

He placed his hands on his hips and studied her. "But it's going to be okay, right? It'll recover and then you're back to competition? I know this is something you've wanted ever since your parents died."

Mia's mouth went dry. She had over the years begun to wonder about that part of her dream. Her parents had died in an accident on the way to a rodeo. She'd been young and that was when her

37

uncle had come to live on the ranch with her. She'd been in fifth grade and for the longest time, she'd not wanted anything to do with riding. She'd even blanked out her ability to ride. But then, later when she'd entered high school a deep desire to connect with her father had overwhelmed her and that was when she'd asked the handsome, quiet cowboy in school to help her relearn what she'd forgotten.

"Yes. It should," she said, a knot of angst twisted in her stomach. She didn't want to think about this right now. Didn't want to discuss the deeper ramifications of her injury and her dreams...dreams being a two edge sword at the moment. She focused on the medical prognosis. "The prognosis is good on a MCL even a tear to the ACL can be overcome with surgery."

"It'll recover. You'll be good as new."

Ty was the hardest working most goal oriented man she'd ever met. He believed if you worked hard enough anything was possible. He should know. He'd told her that when he was in seventh grade he'd started working on a ranch mucking out stalls near his families run-down home. He'd worked hard and soon he was moving up and taking on more and more responsibilities. In the meantime, he spent as much time as possible watching the horse trainer work with the colts. This wasn't something she'd known until he'd told her after they'd become friends.

He'd worked hard, was dedicated to being the best–and now had a growing reputation. The fact that CC had named him in his will said volumes about Ty and his partners.

Yes, Ty was a believer in hard work, dedication and never giving up on a dream.

Was she giving up on a dream or...she let the thought die off because she wasn't ready to go where her thoughts had been going the last few months.

"Sure, it'll be good as new soon," she said. "It's good to be home for a little while. And Uncle Huey really does need me." It was becoming more and more apparent to her that he did.

"I wish I'd realized something was wrong. To be honest, your uncle doesn't come to Mule

Hollow much. He must do all his business in Ranger or one of the smaller towns past him."

"You know how he is. He's so private it hurts." She loved her uncle but she'd often felt isolated by his almost hermit ways.

Ty chuckled. "He is that. Well I guess if we want to meet this deadline and still have time for me to take care of the ranch horses too I'd better get busy. You're welcome to watch."

They headed back to the arena and she watched through the fence encircling the round pen arena. She watched Ty begin to work with the horse.

As good as he was, Ty had his hands full. But the man was patient.

Ever so patient. And after a couple of hours, despite the brisk wind that was picking up and the chill that was starting to intensify in the air it had nothing on the intensity of Ty's attention on the horse.

He had the halter and long lead rope on Sinbad. She watched as he let the skittish horse follow him around the pen. Stepping backwards to get the horse to learn when it was making wrong moves then stepping out again and leading the horse. She watched them work for a while then Ty would reward Sinbad by letting him rest. It was a process that took time and consistency. To someone who had no idea what Ty was doing it would just look like he was doing nothing but moving around and letting the horse follow him or watch him. She knew differently. She'd watched Ty do this many times over the years and others who broke horses naturally. It was a gentle way of building trust with the horse. And it would eventually pay off.

"Sinbad obviously calmed down since yesterday," she said, even after this short of a time seeing a difference in the horse.

Ty spoke softly to Sinbad, halted him then reached out to touch the horse's neck. Sinbad let him. "I'm pleasantly surprised by him. He was a bit overwrought. I'm not sure how he was prior to riding to the auction barn but obviously he wasn't happy about being there yesterday."

"I guess," she said, not sure what to say to that. She'd never been around the horse prior to yesterday so she wasn't sure what its behavior normally was. One thing she did know, she never tired of watching Ty work a horse this way.

Watching Ty in action was mesmerizing to Mia. He had a gift and anyone who watched this knew it.

Her heart was skipping beats on a regular basis by mid-morning when he called the session done.

"That went well. I'm starved. You want to head to Sam's for an early lunch?" He smiled a sexy smile that curled her toes and took her breath.

"Sure," she managed and told herself all the way to his truck to get her head on straight…

But her thoughts were where they did not need to be…thinking about what it would feel like to kiss Ty Calder.

They'd be amazing–*Stop!* She tore her gaze from him and stormed–hobbled more accurately described her graceless race–toward the truck.

She should tell him she couldn't go and instead, she should hop in her truck and get the heck out of there. But no. Nope. She was a twenty-six year old woman who suddenly felt like she was a teenager with her first crush.

But she knew this wasn't a crush. She'd known it for a long time.

He beat her to the white four door truck with the New Horizon Ranch logo inscribed on the side. He opened the passenger door and waited for her to get there.

Tall, lean and oh so perfect—what had she been thinking? She was in one heck of a mess. And as if to show her exactly how much trouble she was in, he popped his hat back off his forehead, cocked his head and shot her another toe-curling grin.

"You sure are slow." His teasing tone warmed her in the cold air.

Whoa girl, just whoa.

"Don't rush me, buster," she said with a shaky laugh, cringing at the wobble in her voice. She was in so much in trouble it hurt. Ty had never looked at her as more than a friend.

"Is something wrong?"

She looked sharply at him at the question. *Oh yeah, big time wrong.* "Nope, nothing," she shot back. *You are a liar and a chicken Mia Shaw.*

Looking at him she knew it was true. But what

was a woman to do?

She had absolutely no idea where to go from here.

CHAPTER FOUR

Mia had always loved the town of Mule Hollow. It was an explosion of color with all the clapboard buildings having been painted different colors when Lacy Brown had driven to town in her 1958 pink convertible Caddy with a vision for marrying off all the cowboys in the dying town. Lacy had joined up with the three older ladies in town who'd started a national ad campaign looking for women to come to Mule Hollow and marry the town cowboys. So far there had been a good many successful marriages in town. Enough to earn the three older ladies the title of the Matchmakin' Posse of Mule Hollow.

Sam's hadn't changed since she'd left. It was still as…atmospheric as always. The walls were made of rough wood paneling that might date back to the time cowboy's rode to town on horseback and guns were strapped to their hips. The tables were made of old scarred wood that had seen many a person gather round it for good food and conversation.

Sam came hustling out of the kitchen, like a man thirty years younger than a man in his early seventies. Not much more than four feet five inches he was a dynamo who loved his job.

She'd just barely gotten through the door when he spotted her.

"Mia! How ya doin' youngin'? It's been forever since I saw you." He pulled her into his arms and gave her a hug.

Though her uncle wasn't much on socializing, Sam was one of his friends. "It's so good to see you. I'm doing okay, Sam."

"What about that thar brace?"

"I bummed my knee up a little but it's going to be fine and I got a trip back home for Christmas in the bargain."

The door of the diner swung open and Applegate Thornton and his buddy Stanley Orr hustled inside. The two older men were like night and day with App, as they called Applegate, being tall, thin and lanky while Stanley was pleasantly plump, and of medium height and jolly.

"Well, look what the cat drug in," App boomed. He and Stanley both were hard of hearing and had been for as long as she could remember. They too were friends with her uncle. But again, unlike his homebody tendency's, these two loved playing checkers at the window table at Sam's where they gave everyone a hard time while keeping tabs on everything going on in Mule Hollow.

After hugs and hellos they all took seats. She and Ty slid into a booth across the aisle from the voracious checker players.

"Hey," App boomed as soon as everyone had gotten settled. "Maybe you can settle this debate for me. I want to be Santa Clause in the Christmas pageant on Friday night." Mia almost spit the water out that she'd just taken into her mouth. App–*Santa*? Impossible.

Wasn't it?

App, bless his heart, was a softie inside who looked like a very crabby sourpuss on the outside. She knew first-hand that he was more bark than bite, he'd helped her uncle out of several financial difficulties over the years. Thinking about that had her questioning again the possibility that her uncle might be in financial trouble now.

She was so glad she'd come home. Family came first and somehow she'd forgotten that. Where he hadn't. He'd always told her to go after her dreams and that he was fine. She'd believed him—now she wondered.

"See thar, finally someone with some sense," App boomed, pulling her attention back to the current situation.

Everyone was staring at her as if she'd lost her mind. "What would it hurt to let him be Santa?" She frowned. They didn't know that App had been her real life Santa when he'd helped her uncle out of a tough time one Christmas. How many other people had he helped out? He might look a little like Scrooge but he wasn't. He had a heart of gold—it was just gruff.

"He'll scare the kids," Stanley chuckled. "They'll run for the hills and be damaged fer life."

"That's right," Sam hooted. "They'll probably need therapy." Sam grinned, teasing his buddy.

Ty's gaze locked onto hers and he smiled. "I agree. Give him a couple of pillows and put him in a suit. He could wear a beard."

"A very thick bushy beard," Stanley grunted and everyone chuckled again.

App had been scowling the whole time and now he shot a couple of sunflower seeds into the big brass spittoon that sat on the floor between him and Stanley. "Y'all are just worthless," he grunted. "Worthless."

Sam laughed. "If Mia says let him be Santa then let him be Santa. It's fine with me if it's fine with you, Stanley. You're the one givin' up the post."

"Heck, I don't mind steppin' down if the kids can take it." He hiked a bushy brow at his friend. "You know when the women hear about this we are not gonna have a moments peace."

App harrumphed. "Norma Sue can just get happy in the same overalls she gets mad in."

"It ain't Norma Sue I'm worried about. Esther Mae is gonna worry us sick. You know how she is about the Christmas pageant."

"How are the ladies? Mia asked.

Norma Sue, Esther Mae and Adela were the infamous "Posse" and pretty much had their thumbs on everything that went on in town.

"They're as ornery as ever," Sam offered. "They're all in a tither getting this program ready. It's their favorite each year. They'll be here for lunch any minute now."

"When they find out you are back home they'll rope you into helping decorate." Ty grinned causing the unsettling and enticing feeling of butterflies to lift inside of Mia again. She needed something to take her mind off of Ty and working on the parade with friends might be the perfect solution.

Spending more time than necessary around Ty would be very unwise until she figured out what she was supposed to do about these feelings that were growing increasingly unavoidable.

Ty had been distracted by Mia all morning. He'd had to force himself to concentrate on Sinbad earlier while Mia watched him work with the horse from the fence. And now he was enjoying the way she lit up the room with her smile. Everyone enjoyed seeing her again and she seemed to be having a great time as well.

"Hey," App said mid-way through the meal. "You were that woman at the auction yesterday wrestling that crazy horse."

Stanley gaped. "Yeah, that was you."

Ty had been wondering if they were going to figure that out.

Mia sighed. "Yes, that was me. Sinbad was behaving badly."

"Ha. We thought you were a gonner fer shor," App admonished her, his frown deepening. "Were you trying to get yourself killed?"

Ty choked on his burger and drew a sharp look from Mia. He held his hands up. "I didn't say anything."

"I loaded the horse so I could have gotten

control at the auction too. Super cowboy had to swoop in and jump into my business."

"He did it just in the nick of time too," Stanley added, not looking any happier than App. "Your uncle know you were doing that?"

"He did. He knew I could handle it."

"Ha," App grunted. "Huey ain't known for his good judgement where cattle and horses are concerned."

"True," Stanley agreed, scowling.

Ty almost felt sorry for her except his fear for her yesterday kept him from going there. She was good with horses but that horse, despite his better behavior today, was unpredictable and dangerous–especially to a woman sporting a knee brace that hindered her quick movement.

"I'm a little insulted here—"

The door of the diner swung open and Mia's words trailed off as a redhead in a violet warm-up suit came hustling inside–Esther Mae Wilcox was always a bright beam of color wherever she went. Behind her the stout ranch woman Norma Sue Jenkins came striding in wearing her ranch coat over her jeans. She wore a pale tan velvet Stetson with a small green sprig of holly with red berries attached to her green hatband.

App and Stanley groaned and Ty had to laugh.

As if the two ladies could sense there was someone new in the diner they zeroed in on Mia like a heat seeking missile. Of course he knew what it was. These were two of the three that made up the posse and the ladies were obsessed. They could sense single females.

"Mia Shaw," Esther Mae exclaimed hustling to their table and launching herself at Mia. She engulfed her into a bear hug that trapped Mia's arms and looked as if it could break Mia's neck from the tight headlock. "It is so good to see you."

"Esther Mae," Norma Sue barked. "You are about to give her whiplash or worse. Let the girl go." The moment Esther Mae released her Norma Sue enveloped her in a suffocating hug.

Mia lived through the hugging and was laughing when the women backed up and grinned at her. "Now you ladies know how to make a girl feel welcomed home." She laughed and shot disgruntled eyes at App and Stanley.

"We try," Esther Mae replied.

Norma Sue nodded agreement about the time Adela entered the diner. "Come see who is eating lunch with Ty," she called to Sam's small, elegant wife.

"*Mia*, what a wonderful surprise. Sam and I have been hoping you would come home to have Christmas with Huey. He's been so lonesome."

Mia looked a little startled. "I had suspected it when I talked with him on the phone and he's been really quiet ever since I arrived home."

Ty realized she was worried. Huey always did have his peculiarities–but then Ty knew he was fairly quiet himself. He figured Mia's uncle would talk when the mood hit him…it obviously just hadn't hit him. Still, Ty would ask Mia if there was anything he could do to help even if he seriously doubted there was. And so lunch went until finally Mia checked her watch and said she needed to get home. By that time Mia had been roped into helping with the last bit of decorating and so had Ty.

He wasn't so blind that he couldn't imagine what they were up to. He knew exactly why the ladies couldn't stop smiling as they chattered from the booth behind his and Mia's. They'd asked Mia about her injury and how long she was going to be home. Mia told them exactly what she'd told him—she'd be here over the Christmas holiday. After that it depended on her leg.

That gave Ty a small window of time. He had until New Year's Eve to win Mia's heart.

CHAPTER FIVE

"What do you mean you're leaving?" Mia asked, staring at her uncle. Shockwaves reverberated through her. She'd arrived back at their ranch to find him packing things into a rundown hatchback. And there was an older woman, maybe in her sixties...maybe older. It was hard to tell under all her red lipstick. There was enough of that to paint the barn and it was smeared–but from the look of Uncle Huey, he'd been the cause of that. On top of that the woman had a nervous twitch in her left eye and the fake eyelash on that eye had come unglued at the edge and kept waving at Mia with every twitch.

"Mia, I'm sorry, honey, but I'm moving. It's time and Earline and me, we love each other. And she's come all the way from her pig farm in the panhandle to fetch me." He put his weight into stuffing the last bag into the back end of the car and then yanked the hatchback shut.

Mia could only watch in dismay. Was he serious? He'd been acting odd but this was absolutely shocking. She tried to speak but nothing came out. She tried again, "But," her voice cracked. "Um, how did y'all meet?" She wasn't sure what to do in a situation like this. He was a grown man...

He grinned—no—beamed as he wrapped an arm around Earline's waist and tugged her close. Earline was taller than him by three inches and looked down at him with adoring eyes.

"We met on that matchmaking website for farmers," he said. "I took one look at her photo and the rest is history. I went out to her place for a little while you were gone and then came home. But, honey, I can't deny it any longer. I love Earline and I am gonna make her my wife. It don't mean I don't love you, Mia. Because I do, honey. And I've tried to be here for you." He looked love-struck as he gazed up into Earline's adoring eyes.

"It's time to get on with my life. You're going to be fine."

Mia's heart turned over at the conviction in his voice and in both their eyes. "Yes, sure. I'll be fine." Was she hearing this correctly? "But–so you just met recently?"

"Naw," he laughed. "We've been talking now for four months and like I said I went out there last month for a couple of days until I got worried about my responsibilities…but I can't go on this way."

"I got real worried about him," Earline said. "So I had to come check on him. I told him last night that I was coming."

Uncle Huey looked up at her adoringly. "And she came to me."

"I couldn't help myself, pookie," Earline rasped. "I stayed away as long as I could."

Uncle Huey grinned wide enough to swallow the Grand Canyon. "And I'm glad you came after me. I've been moping around here long enough by myself. I need you, Earline."

Mia groaned inside. Despite being in total and

complete shock the tender touch of true affection bubbling out of her uncle dug deep. Her uncle had been lonely.

For as long as she'd known him he'd been alone. In his quiet little world. Yes, he adored her and she knew that, but deep down she sensed so much missing from his life.

He shot her a glance finally. "The place is yours, Mia, not mine. I've just been taking care of it for you because you needed me to. Your daddy wanted me to take care of you if he couldn't be here to do that and I was honored to do it... But, honey, you're old enough now and I've finally gotten my chance at happiness...so I'm takin' it."

Mia's heart clutched as he gave a lovelorn look at Earlette or was it Elvira? Mia was so overwhelmed she couldn't think straight.

"I'm not asking you to not go," she managed. "But maybe you need to think—"

"I don't need to think about it. I've been thinking about it for four long months now and I don't want to waste another minute. I've been waiting on Earline all my life. Now that I've found her I ain't aiming to lose her. I'm goin'. I love you, girl, but Earline is my soulmate and she needs me now."

Earline peered earnestly at Mia. "I love your uncle so much. And we're going to be real happy. Maybe you can come up for Christmas in a couple of weeks. I've plenty of room in my old rambler of a house."

What was she supposed to say? Mia could not stand in the way of her uncle's happiness and he was happier now than she'd ever seen him. But he'd met this woman on the Internet. Shouldn't he learn more about her before running off with her?

"Okay, we got to go. It's a long drive to Vegas."

"*Vegas*?" Mia's antenna flew to attention. "What do you mean Vegas?"

"We're getting married."

"But...Oh," Mia squeaked. Her uncle came forward then and wrapped his arms around her and gave her a hard hug.

"You're going to be alright, young lady. Do what you want with the place. Keep it or sell it and make your dreams come true. I'm fixin' ta go after mine now. I guess you could say we're eloping."

Tears welled in her eyes. He had the right. He'd given up his own life and moved here after her parents died in order to take care of her. All she could do now was to be happy for him and let him go. She hugged him tight. "I love you, Uncle Huey. Take care—" before she could finish he'd released her and with a hurried smile he ushered Earline to the car. Mia watched as Earline and her leopard print spandex disappeared inside the passenger side of the car and then her uncle, grinning like a kid, hustled around and jumped in behind the wheel. The car cranked up and with a sputter and a hiccup carried her uncle away and left Mia standing in a cloud of exhaust. The last thing she saw was Uncle Huey's arm waving out the driver's side window at her.

She coughed and watched with watery eyes as the man who'd always been there for her drove away.

Suddenly brake lights came on and then, the car backed up. Her uncle had come to his senses. Mia wiped tears from her eyes as Uncle Huey's door opened and he came hurrying back to her. His smile lit his entire face.

"Mia, honey, I almost forgot." He tugged a piece of paper from his shirt pocket. "Here is where you can find me. This is Earline's address and you know my cell number." He pressed the paper into her hands and then frowned. "Don't look so sad. Aren't you happy for me?""W-well yes, I'm just worried."

"Worried," he scoffed. "There's no need to worry. And besides, I'm very capable of taking care of myself. Be happy for me."

She nodded and hugged him tight once more. "It's just, sudden, you know."

"But it's right for me." He gave her arms a squeeze and a serious glint came into his eyes and then he strode back to his car and drove away.

"What do you mean he just left?" Ty had received a call from a very distressed Mia and had immediately stopped what he was doing and driven out to see her.

Worry etched her expression.

"He's been acting strange every time I talked to him on the phone for the last few months. He's been forgetful and distracted. I thought something was going on and I've been very worried. I knew I needed to come home even before I got hurt but I didn't."

"Mia, you were on a mission. He understood that. He always supported you in reaching for your dream."

Her forehead crinkled. "But, he was always here for me and I haven't been here for him. This is all my fault—"

"Whoa. Mia, he's a grown man. You are not responsible for this." He put his hands on her shoulders and squeezed gently. "Slow down and breathe, honey."

Her wide eyes held his as she nodded then inhaled. "He eloped, Ty. Eloped. I wasn't even invited to the wedding. I barely got to meet Earline."

He knew this was a blow to her. "I think your uncle was so excited about what he was doing that he hasn't even realized he might have hurt your feelings by not inviting you to the wedding." He could tell she was struggling and he wondered if she even realized how expressive her facial features were.

"It was just such a shock. He was here and then he was gone. Just like that."

He could only imagine how she felt. His own parents had moved to Florida a few years earlier and were having the time of their life. He'd never lost one of them. That had to be especially hard on a young kid.

"He loaded his stuff up and told me it was his turn to be happy. And then he drove away in a puff of smoke."

"He has a point."

Her eyes narrowed. "He met her on some online dating site. Which is fine, I have friends who are happily married after meeting online but…well, he never said anything before. It seems to have come out of nowhere."

Ty massaged her tense shoulders, trying to calm her as he rolled the conversation over in his mind.

"The truth is he's a grown man."

Fire danced in her eyes. "Yes, he is. But what if he's having issues that I'm not aware of because I wasn't around? You know, maybe he's showing signs of compromised thoughts? Onset of some problem?"

"I get that. But, if you're worried you can go out there and check on him. Mia, he's done nothing wrong. And you can't start blaming yourself for something that is out of your control."

"But—" she moved away from him.

"Mia, for now maybe you should stop worrying about Huey and let him try to find his own way while you find your own way. If he's made a mistake he can always come back here, right?"

She nodded.

He gave her a smile. "That's what I thought. So the best thing you can do is try to figure out a plan of what you need to do. Let Huey have this time, be happy for him. And *you* enjoy your Christmas holiday. "

Mia searched his gaze with conflicted eyes, her expression pensive. Finally, she nodded. "You're absolutely right. It's just that ever since I lost my parents he's been there for me. And even when I was on the road I always knew he was here. Yes, its selfish sounding but I feel lost with him not being here."

He watched her as she gazed around the office. "He was your grounding stone even though you weren't here that much."

"Yes. But, he has a right to a life too. He deserves the chance to make his own way. Even if it's a mistake. I hope it's not. I pray it is wonderful. And that he's happy. He does deserve it."

Ty pulled her into his arms for an impulsive hug. Tugging her to him, he held her close and was startled when she came easily, as if she needed it as much as he did. "I'm doing the same. And I'm here if you need me."

She felt so amazing in his arms. Her head rested momentarily on his shoulder and her arms were draped easily around his waist. He resisted the urge to hold her closer and press a kiss against her temple…or her lips. He was grateful that he was a pretty restrained kind of guy or he might have messed up royally.

"Thank you," she whispered.

He felt her face move and he looked down to find her looking up at him, his heart dropped and his mouth went dry. His gaze moved to her slightly parted lips—

"I better go," he blurted out and let her go as he backed toward the door. "Call if you need me."

In a rush he strode out of the office and out of the house. The cold blast of air was welcomed as it swept across his heated skin. He had to fight the need to turn around and go back in there and tell Mia exactly how he felt. But that was the last thing she needed now.

No, what she needed now was a friend. And only a friend. Exposing his feelings to her at this point and time would only be selfish on his part.

He got in his truck and headed for safety. A few miles down the road he found himself smiling as he thought of reclusive Uncle Huey tossing his fears aside and taking a risk for love.

"Way to go, Huey," he said out loud. "Way to go, buddy."

CHAPTER SIX

"So, what's up between you and Mia," Dalton asked the next morning.

"Nothing," he shrugged and shot a glance across the street toward Mia.

He and Dalton had been designated to help decorate while Rafe and Chase oversaw ranch business today. Maddie was helping too and she was across the street with Mia and a herd of women including Norma Sue and Esther Mae who were ramrodding the decorations. Adela was there too but she wasn't as vocal as her friends.

Ty was curious if Mia had opened up to the ladies and he planned to ask Maddie later if she had. Mia and Maddie would make good friends and he hoped so, Mia needed someone she could relate to and since both his partner and Mia were horse women maybe they'd connect. He hoped she would find a friend.

He and Dalton were standing on top of the Heavenly Inspirations Hair Salon hanging wreaths among the lights down Main Street. The town had been decorated for three weeks, with lights so thick a satellite would think the town of four hundred was the size of Houston. It was pretty though, he couldn't deny that.

"C'mon, what's going on?" Dalton prodded, looking unconvinced.

Ty busied himself tightening the tie strap that would hold the wreath to the bannister that edged the salon's roof. From beneath his hat brim he could see Mia across the street from him wrapping another strand of lights around the window of Pete's Feed and Seed. She was bundled up like everyone else in a coat and a scarf that almost hid her face. Looking at her, Ty didn't feel the chill but felt pure warmth radiate through him.

"That much," Dalton said, amusement in his tone.

Ty slung his gaze to his friend. They were the

last of the partners not married so far and he and
Dalton had been close from the first day Dalton
had shown up at the ranch, barely three years ago.
"Is it that evident?"

Dalton grimaced. "Afraid so, buddy. So what's
the story, you've never mentioned her."

"I didn't see a need to talk about something
that I never saw any hope in. I never expected her
to come home. I figured she'd reach her goals and
move on to bigger and better things than this tiny
town."

"But now she's back." Dalton finished
attaching the wreath he was working on. "So
how'd y'all meet?"

Ty told him about how shy he'd been and how
he couldn't talk to her and then because Dalton
was a good friend he told him everything.

"Wow," he said, when Ty finished. "So she has
no idea you're in love with her?"

"None." He'd kept his silly Christmas wish to
himself because it was so unlike him to wish
something like that. A man could only go so far
before his buddies thought he was a complete sap.

"You need to tell her. Really, Ty. I'm not jumping on the marriage bandwagon like all our other partners and I thought you were going to hang onto your single status with me but…man, if you love her you need to let her know."

She happened to look his direction in that moment, almost as if she knew they were talking about her. He smiled and she reciprocated. Her simple smile from three hundred feet away warmed him. She looked tired this morning and he wondered how long she stayed up worrying about her uncle.

"Yeah, I plan to." He needed to tell her how he felt before he made a mistake and kissed her.

"You've got it bad," Dalton grunted. "Come on, let's get this finished before you fall off this roof and hurt yourself."

Ty laughed. "Keep that between the two of us, okay."

"Buddy, if you looked in the mirror you would see that it's not me who has the look of a lovesick pup written all over his face. I don't need to tell anyone."

71

Ty scowled. "Give it up, I'm a great poker player."

Dalton just laughed. "In your dreams, partner."

Mia concentrated on attaching the garland to the window frame. She'd almost not come to help the ladies decorate. She'd tried not to worry about her uncle but she couldn't help herself and she'd had a hard night. She'd finally given up trying to sleep and gotten up and made coffee. She'd watched the sun rise while sipping the hot brew and prayed that the Lord would give her some direction on her life. She'd realized that she and Uncle Huey had had something in common over the last few years…they'd both been growing increasingly unhappy with where their life was heading. Uncle Huey had taken control—at least it would seem so—and now had taken steps to alter his future and his happiness. Adela had been excited for Uncle Huey and had gone immediately to tell Sam.

Adela's reaction had helped Mia feel more positive about her uncle's sudden direction change for his life. But could Mia do it?

"That Ty Calder can't take his eyes off of you," Esther Mae said with a lilt and an elbow to Mia's arm.

Mia shot a startled glance over her shoulder to where Ty was climbing down a ladder across the street. She'd fought not to watch him all morning. Her mouth went dry every time she looked at him and she thought about him holding her in his arms the night before.

She shivered as a new burst of chilled air hit her–looking at Ty every once in a while had helped keep her warm.

"He's probably worried about me," she offered. Trying to diffuse the interest that was obvious in Esther Mae's observation. But deep down knowing he was watching her had her stomach turning over with nerves.

"The posse tells me you and Ty go way back," Lacy Matlock said. It was a statement rather than a question.

Mia's alarms went off at the nickname Esther Mae and her two buddies had earned. She looked at the blonde salon owner and hoped this wasn't a signal that the matchmakin' posse had zoomed in on her. She had enough problems without that, though she knew the truth…and a quick glance at the expectant and bright eyed look on Esther Mae's face confirmed her suspicion.

"Well…yes we do," she fumbled, then added in a rush. "I mean we are friends. Have been—since school." Her answers were choppy from the nervousness that had slammed into her. She glanced around the group helping with the decorating of the feed store. Esther Mae, Adela and Norma Sue plus Lacy were all smiles now.

Esther Mae held a box with sprigs of greenery tied with red ribbon and two silver bells. Now she picked one out of the box and waved it in the air causing the two bells to tinkle as she smiled mischievously.

Mistletoe.

She was waving mistletoe at Mia.

Mia gave a dry laugh, seeing the way the posse's eyes lit up—it was enough to give her an ulcer.

"This is going to be stationed all over the

place," Esther Mae cooed.

"So get that cowboy under it. He's been single for a very long time," Norma Sue added. "Ever since high school and I have always wondered why." Speculation filled her eyes as they darted from Mia to Ty who'd just started toward them from across the street. He looked every inch the irresistible cowboy.

"Y'all, we're just friends," Mia blurted out. "He just hasn't found the right one." Why was she fighting this? These women could be her allies if she chose to use them. But, that just seemed wrong to her. She knew her cheeks were probably beaming like a Christmas tree. "He's just barely turned thirty. There's no rush—"

"No rush for what?" Ty asked sauntering up at that inopportune moment.

Mia groaned. Her newly forming ulcer started hurting.

"Mia was just telling us you aren't in any hurry to get married," Norma said.

Adela chuckled as she carried a poinsettia to the flower pot outside the feed store doors. She looked at Ty. "I don't think you should rush either. But certainly never swear off marriage. You haven't done that have you, Ty?"

Ty looked confused and no wonder, the poor man had walked up innocent as a lamb and been drawn into some bizarre conversation about him and marriage. It was hilarious and scary to Mia at the same time.

"No, ma'am, I haven't given swearing off marriage much thought. I figured it would happen when it happened."

Esther Mae let out a gleeful squeal. "Wonderful! I love a man who thinks like that. So you aren't broken-hearted or anything like that? I was afraid some young woman from school had broken your heart and you'd never recovered or something horrible like that."

Mia caught a flicker of something in Ty's eyes...it hit her hard and took her breath away as she suddenly realized that maybe Esther Mae was onto something. Had Ty been in love? But with who?

Ty's gray eyes shadowed darker and he didn't

say anything at first. Which really meant Esther Mae might be right. Ty had been in love and never gotten over it. And maybe that was why he'd grown so distant from her over the last few years. He'd met someone and then lost her.

And all the while she was out there riding her horse and chasing dreams. Empty dreams she was starting to think.

The thought was so far away from anything she'd ever considered that she was speechless. Time had continued here in Mule Hollow while she'd been gone.

What had she been thinking? That this handsome, amazing man would never fall in love?

She waited for him to deny it and though he looked caught off guard he didn't deny it either.

If a guy had never been in love he would deny it—*right?*

Mia needed space. Now. "Well, I'm done here," she said. "I'm freezing. I think I have to go get some coffee." She was proud that she didn't stutter or stumble over her words but thankful that if she had of done so, she could blame it on the cold and not the shock.

Her feet felt heavy as she urged them to move. The bad thing was that Ty was standing between her and Sam's.

She was overreacting, but numb with cold. Why wasn't anyone else as cold as she was? It was like she'd just frozen up on the inside.

Ty looked relieved that she'd changed the subject. "That's actually why I came over. I wanted to see if you, or any of you ladies, needed a warm beverage."

The expressions of delight on the group's faces could not be denied. They gaped with glee at the fact that he had asked them if they wanted something to drink...or, it hit her like a brick to the forehead that they could also be excited because she was about to go get coffee and so was Ty.

Matchmaking at its finest.

"On second thought, I believe I'll go home now and really get warm. I—"

"No!" The three ladies exclaimed in unison and Lacy hooted with laughter.

Esther Mae came forward holding her back.

"We were supposed to go pick out a Christmas tree but…if you two young folks want to brave the elements instead of making me and my old bones go out there then I'm not going to gripe. And Norma Sue has older bones than mine—"

"My bones are just fine," Norma Sue barked, shooting her buddy a scowl. "I've hoisted more baby calves up onto the backs of horses and brought them home through freezing rain than most cowboys have in their lifetime–thank you very much. Matter of fact, I've got a baby calf waiting to be fed this afternoon so y'all getting the tree would be very helpful."

Adela blinked big, blue eyes at Mia and Ty and smiled kindly. "You could leave the truck running as you look and it shouldn't take too much time."

Ty hitched a perfect dark brow at Mia. "Do you have time to do this? I don't mind. Sounds fun."

Fun. Sure, if you liked to torture yourself. "Sure. I'd love to help out." She had visions of old movies where the two love interests wander romantically through the trees looking for the perfect tree and they kiss and…oh, the torture of it all. She was beginning to lose her mind. Yup, she was indeed.

Of course her saying yes brought huge grins and smiles of relief and she had a feeling there would be some high-fives as soon as she and Ty drove out of town.

"Great." Ty's warm eyes twinkled appealingly and set the butterflies into an uproar inside her chest. "But first, let's get you that coffee."

Coffee? What coffee…Mia had forgotten all about the coffee.

CHAPTER SEVEN

They chose to go to Ty's ranch because he knew the perfect spot. An area that had a lot of cedar trees with perfect Christmas tree potential.

As they rode through the pasture Mia chewed on her lower lip and studied the brewing storm clouds. "Those clouds look ominous."

"I think the snow is going to happen—might even get here just in time for the pageant. I'm just hoping we miss the freeze. If the temperature drops too low and the freeze comes in then everything will get cancelled."

"For everyone's sake, I'm dreamin' of a white Christmas and nothing more," Mia said. "I loved that old movie." The thought of snow right now sounded as romantic to her as that old movie had been. Of course at the moment being in the truck with Ty made everything romantic to her.

Her nerves were shot and if she wasn't careful she could make a fool of herself.

Think thoughts of freezing temperatures and billowing ice storms...

Ty looked over at her and every ounce of the icy blizzard she'd just conjured up melted away in a heat flash. *Drats.*

"Are you alright?" Ty asked, studying her.

"I'm fine. Why wouldn't I be?"

"You look kind of flustered." He looked back out the window and she looked straight ahead too.

Snow. Talk about snow. She rubbed her temple and tried to sound casual, "If it would stick that would be lovely. Snow that is. Although I was in the Denver area last year and got snowed in and my truck and trailer got stuck on the side of the road. It was not a fun experience. I thought I would freeze and thankfully a couple of really nice guys stopped to help me."

Ty looked at her sharply, his gaze narrowed. "It scares me, you being on the road like that all alone. That could have been a really dangerous situation."

"It actually was and I'll admit that I said a few prayers that God would send the right person to help me." She didn't add that she'd been terribly frightened at the time. Dark had been creeping up on her and she hadn't known what she was going to do. There had been no phone service in that stretch of road and she was smart enough to admit that she could have been in trouble. "The Lord looked out for me and sent two very nice men along to help."

"Still, it was dangerous."

She had mixed feelings about his concern. It felt nice to know he was concerned for her but also a little annoying…she had been on the road alone for four years. She didn't need him pointing out to her that this had been a dangerous situation.

"I've been taking care of myself for a long time, Ty," she pointed out. His expression grew tighter and he gave a quick nod then got out of the truck. She did the same. She was a little confused by his behavior as she started following him toward the trees.

The wind had picked up and it howled as it

wove between the pines. Ty spun unexpectedly and Mia slammed hard against him. Instantly, his hands were on her arms.

"Whoa, are you alright?"

She nodded. More than a little aware of how close she was to him. That there was a mere breath between them as he gently gripped her arms. "I'm fine." Her breath came in white puffs in the cold air. And it could have been because she was suddenly warm all over.

His fingers tightened on her arms and he studied her as if…he might be thinking about kissing her. Mia had now gone from wanting something to imagining things that weren't there.

He swallowed and then blinked hard. "Mia—"

For self-preservation she moved away from him. "W-why were you acting like that back there?" she asked, refocusing on what had happened moments ago.

Looking puzzled he didn't say anything for a moment. "I got overprotective for a minute."

"Ty, I've been away for a long time and suddenly I come home and you're feeling

84

protective." She was being rude and she knew it. But…well, picking a fight was self-preservation! "I know you're independent and strong and can take care of yourself. But I do get worried about you sometimes. That's what friends do."

He worried about her. As a friend, she reminded herself. She needed that reminder so her imagination wouldn't get carried away. Really, she was a grown woman for goodness sakes.

"Right," she said easily. "I'm fine. Always have been." She swallowed hard as her gaze rested on his lips.

"You're freezing. Your cheeks are ruby red." He touched her cheek and she had to fight not to lean into that touch like a kitten getting scratched behind the ears.

She moved out away from his touch. "We better get this tree cut down."

"Right. Come on, let's get this tree and get you out of this weather." He turned back and led the way toward the trees again.

Disappointment dug a hole in her heart but she fought it off. She was tougher than this.

Suddenly, three deer ran from the trees in front of them making their graceful dash toward a stand of trees in the distance. Mia gasped and watched them race down the slope, their short white tails bobbing with each step.

It gave her a moment to focus on something else. "They're beautiful. And so are these trees," she forced her voice to sound normal.

"Why don't we get you a tree while we're here also?"

"I don't know..." Mia really wasn't sure she was in the mood for a tree.

"Come on, Mia. You need a tree. I know with your uncle leaving like he did that you might feel abandoned for Christmas. But you need a tree. And if it helps at least a little, well, I'm here and I'm going to make certain you are not alone for the holidays."

How had he done that? Read her inner thoughts so well? She hadn't wanted to admit completely that her uncle's leaving had doused her Christmas spirit. But it was undeniable and Ty had seen it.

He smiled temptingly and she couldn't help smiling back. "It's true. Is it that obvious that I was struggling?"

"Not so much. Maybe I'm just able to read you."

That made her smile widen and her heart turn over. If he only knew. "Maybe so."

"So how about that tree?"

"A small one would be great. With my knee I don't really feel like decorating a big one."

"I'll help you decorate. And since you are going to be alone for Christmas I'm hoping you'll join me and my partners at the big house for Christmas dinner. We'd love to have you join us. You can meet everyone."

Mia wished he'd said he wanted her to join him but he'd said us.

Us.

Oh how that word could mean so much more. Us as in him and her would be wonderful but it was us as in the group and clearly did not mean what her heart was wishing for... What was she doing?

Trying to get her heart broken? And now that Uncle Huey had left her, Mia was facing another problem...deep in her heart of hearts she wasn't sure she could take one more person in her life leaving her alone. It would be much easier on her to just leave. Wouldn't it?

Ty studied Mia. Something was going on behind those pretty but hesitant eyes of hers. Maybe she wasn't sure she wanted to be around him for Christmas. Something was certainly wrong. "You don't have to if you don't want to. It's completely up to you."

She shivered in the cold, but finally her pretty lips lifted into a smile. "No, sorry. Christmas with all of your friends sounds like a lot of fun. I'd love to join y'all. Thank you for asking." She wasn't fooling him, something was still wrong. "My pleasure. Everyone is looking forward to meeting you. You met Dalton earlier and Maddie too, but her husband Cliff will be there along with his twin, Rafe and his wife Sadie. And Chase and his fiancé

Amber will be there too. It'll be a good sized group." He could tell she was freezing so he started moving again. It was either that or wrap her up in his arms and kiss her till she was warm. He had kissing on his mind and he knew it. "Let's find that tree and get you out of this cold."

She didn't argue.

They spent the next thirty minutes wandering through the cold in search of the perfect tree.

"Oh, it's snowing!" Mia exclaimed as huge snowflakes suddenly began to drift gently down on them. She laughed and looked up into the falling snowflakes.

Ty knew he'd never seen anything so beautiful. His heart hammered like a thousand horses watching her.

She laughed. "I've seen snow everywhere and driven through snowstorms and yet when it snows here in our corner of the world I get so excited." She turned with her arms held out and let the flakes settle on her.

"I think it's the ease factor. When we get snow here in central Texas it's special and not heavy enough to linger and make a mess. It comes softly then leaves softly."

She stared at him now with a quizzical expression. "Wow, you said that so perfectly, Mr. Horse Whisperer."

He chuckled. "I'm trying." The snow dusted her hair and her shoulders now and was coming down thicker by the second. She looked heavenward again and laughed, holding her palms outstretched she turned in a slow motion, being careful of her knee. Ty had to do everything in his power to keep his distance.

She stopped suddenly. "There. That's it." She pointed at a large perfect tree sitting on the edge of the hill. Snowflakes dusted the cedar tree emphasizing its shape perfectly.

Mia's expression was joyful as she pulled her jacket close and looked from the tree to him. "What do you think?"

"Perfect," he said, his voice gruff. "I'll get the saw." He spun and high-tailed it away from her as fast as he could. It was either that or him doing something he might regret; like taking her into his arms and claiming her soft lips with his.

Like exposing his heart when the time wasn't right.

Too much was at stake for him to mess up now.

CHAPTER EIGHT

"What do you mean you haven't told him?"

Mia bit her lip and fought down the frustration eating away inside of her as she held the phone to her ear and listened to her friend Kara Mosey on the other end of the line. Kara was a barrel racer on the circuit and had been Mia's friend for years.

"Look, Kara, I can't tell him. I'm back here and things between us are right back like they used to be…it's comfortable. Sort of. If I tell him, I might put some really uncomfortable vibes between us and everything could fall apart."

There was a long, loud, very exasperated sigh that could be heard clearly on Mia's end of the phone.

"Come on, Kara, give me some understanding

here. You're all I've got."

"That's just it, Mia. There's more to life than just pining away for a guy. There's an actual relationship and a future. You need more than just me. I'm not good with relationships but then, I'm not the one in love with a guy and afraid to admit it. I'm fine being alone—because I'm not in love with someone. You are, babe, and it's time to admit it. You deserve to have him. And by the way, comfortable is not really living. You used to have some fire to you."

Mia rubbed the goal post that had formed in between her eyes. "I'll tell him. But this is too important to mess up and so it's got me feeling and acting strange. I don't know what's wrong with me."

"You're in love with a man and you've been holding it in too long, girlfriend. Let it free."

"You're right. I'm not a mouse. I'm an independent woman who goes after what she wants." But did she want to risk loving someone and them rejecting her or the possibility that they would eventually leave. Not putting herself at risk was easier.

Safer.

"That's my girl. You go get that hunk of good looking cowboy."

Mia gave a half-hearted chuckle. She'd been moping around the house ever since they cut down the Christmas trees two days ago and it wasn't doing her any favors. She had told Ty that she had to go over the books some more and get everything sorted out. This had given her the excuse not to go check on how he was progressing with Sinbad—besides she knew he was capable of taming that horse without her input. He'd offered to help her decorate the tree but she'd said she could do it. She glanced at the tree in the corner.

It sat exactly where he'd placed it two days ago.

"So, are you going to the pageant that y'all cut the tree down for?"

"Yes, I'm going. The town is supposed to be lit up and the Christmas pageant is a small production with a live nativity scene with live animals—including the most adorable donkey named Samantha. I've been around that little donkey and love watching her with the kids. She's practically human. There's also supposed to be campfires for everyone to gather around and roast marshmallows while singing Christmas carols with the cowboys. I haven't been here since they started doing these and it just sounds like the most fun—" she stopped talking when Kara's chuckling interrupted her.

"What?" she asked.

"You. You sound happier right now than you've sounded in the last year and a half. Heck maybe the last four years. You love it there in that town. I'm not saying that I agree with you dropping out of the competition next year, but right now you sound good. You should talk to Ty and tell him what's going on. Tell him everything. Give him a chance to be your guy."

Her guy. She liked the sound of that.

Ty was running late coming into town. He'd had a horse that might be foaling tonight and he'd had to get her settled into the stall before he left. He wouldn't be here long so he searched for Mia. He had kept his distance since they'd cut down the Christmas trees. But he'd been distracted thinking about her. Something was wrong with Mia, he was sure of it.

"Yoo-hoo, Ty," Esther Mae called from her position at the end of the sidewalk near the nativity scene. She was decked out in a red velvet dress, a white apron and a heavy green cape that draped over her shoulders to help ward off the cold air. A white bonnet partially covered her red hair. She was extremely colorful as she waved him over through the crowd.

"Don't you look nice this evening," he said. "Are you Mrs. Clause?"

She grinned mischievously. "Are you kidding? Santa is App and even though it's pretend, I will not be pretending something like that. I'm actually Mrs. *Mistletoe*. I've been very busy this week sneaking mistletoe all over town." She winked at him. "So be watchful, young man. It might come in handy."

He chuckled. "I think you're the first Mrs.

Mistletoe that I've ever met."

"I thought this up myself. Hey, Norma look who I found," she called.

Norma Sue hustled down the boardwalk like a woman on a mission. Ty instantly braced himself as her gaze locked onto him.

The robust ranch woman clapped him on the shoulder. "You and Mia sure did pick us out a great tree. It's down the street in the community center where Santa is set up. You should go see it. Mia is down there. I think she's serving punch to the kids."

Did he have a sign on his chest that said he was looking for Mia?

Esther Mae cocked her bonneted head and grinned. "And remember, I've put mistletoe everywhere." She leaned toward him conspiratorially. "Even places you would not suspect—so keep an eye out for it."

"Ah, okay," he said, and took a step toward anywhere but there. "You ladies have a great evening."

Norma Sue pushed her Stetson back off her

forehead, exposing her bushy gray curls. "We're trying to. Bring Mia back by for some marshmallows and hot chocolate. You two can sing Christmas carols together."

Okay, so there was no getting around the fact that he and Mia had bulls-eyes on them. Ty had managed for over four years to avoid having this happen. These ladies weren't your average matchmakers–not that he kept up with them all that much but it was a known fact that if they connected you with someone things were going to happen. And those "things" involved walking down the church aisle.

So that was a good thing, right?

Ty gave them a tight smile. "I've got a mare I'm keeping watch on tonight so I'll be heading out pretty soon. I just thought I'd come to town and see the festivities for a short time. And it looks like y'all have a great turnout despite the cold temperature.""Makes for some good snuggling weather." Esther Mae looked delighted about the cold air. "I tell you what, me and my Hank, we still like to snuggle by a good ole campfire."

Ty did have to admit that both Norma Sue and Esther Mae had marriages that still seemed to have spark to them. Though he knew both men pretty much let their wives get a little too heavy in the matchmaking role, he figured they knew when they were fighting a losing battle.

He did too as he wished them a good night again and got out of there as quick as possible—and he didn't go directly to the community center.

Nope, he felt them watching him and he tried to throw them off his track by heading across the street to speak to a few friends. Then he made his way down that side of town and back across the street to slip into the community center. Sure they would know he was here but it didn't hurt to make them wonder. He felt pretty silly, but he was a fairly low-keyed person and being watched and set up made him about as uncomfortable as it got.

The minute he entered the building he felt the energy of the room. Excited kids were everywhere. The room was roaring with laughter and chatter and squeals of delight as kids ran and played while waiting to see Applegate Thornton aka Santa

Clause.

From the doorway he had a straight shot at the older man's expression and despite the bushy white beard, the fluffy white wig and Santa cap App wore, it was apparent that he was grinning like a peacock. And to Ty's surprise Stanley had dressed up like a big elf and was helping his buddy make kiddos smile.

Awesome.

And then he found Mia in the crowd and his heart surged with love. She was helping a group of ladies at a table handing out bags of candy to the kids and she was all smiles.

He headed that way and had to fight not to swing her up into his arms. Boy, that would get some attention.

"Hey there," he said. "You look like you're having fun." She looked up and he saw a flare of something in her eyes that warmed his heart when she saw him.

"I've had a great time. Want to help?" She handed him a bag of candy and pointed at the next kid in line.

Ty handed the smiling boy the candy.

"Thanks, mister," the kid exclaimed as he took the candy then ran off to his mom a few feet away.

"You having fun?" he asked her.

"Oh yes. Not only is it warm in here, it's fun to be a part of making the kids smile. I love the nativity program going on outside too. Jesus truly is the reason for the season but watching children playing and laughing makes me happy too."

"I agree." She looked a lot more relaxed than she'd looked two days ago after he'd delivered her tree to her. She'd been anxious to get rid of him and hadn't let him help decorate the tree like he'd thought they were going to do.

More the reason to move slow and helping her hand out candy now was perfect. And so they spent the next half hour standing beside each other handing out treats to bright faced children and watching App and Stanley have the time of their lives listening to children's Christmas wishes.

The door opened about an hour later and Sadie and Maddie came into the room. They spotted him and came straight over.

"Hey, Ty," Sadie said, smiling huge as she looked from him to Mia. "So this is where you're hiding out."

"Yeah, I was—" he started but Maddie broke him off.

"Sadie this is Mia," she said, grinning big as the state of Texas. "The one I was telling you about who helped decorate the town a couple of days ago."

Sadie chuckled. "Well, yes, I already figured that out." She held her hand out to Mia. "Sadie Masterson, I'm married to Rafe. He's one of the partners out at the ranch."

"And my husband Cliff's twin brother," Maddie added. They were both now looking from Ty to Mia with excited, assessing eyes.

"I'm glad to meet you both," Mia said, filling another cup of punch for a small girl who immediately ran away, sloshing some of her drink as she ran. Mia smiled. "She won't have much left to drink if she's not more careful."

"Thank you for volunteering for this," Sadie said. "We're actually here to relieve you. It's our turn to have some fun and you two crazy kids need to go roast a marshmallow or something." She smiled broadly.

"You're coming for Christmas dinner, right?" Maddie asked.

"If you have room for me," Mia said, glancing at him.

"Oh, we have room," Maddie said, her eyes were twinkling and Ty's stomach knotted.

They all talked for a little longer and then gave up their posts.

"How about a quick cup of hot chocolate before I call it a night. I need to check on a mare," he asked her as he helped her put on her thick coat.

"I'd love some. Is something wrong with the mare?" They walked out onto the sidewalk and paused to let several families with children pass by.

He liked the concern in her voice. He told her about the mare he thought would foal later on that night. "Is the vet coming out?"

"Na, I'm pretty experienced in helping if something goes wrong. But it's going to be fine. If

I was worried I wouldn't be here at all."

Mia looked thoughtful. "Would you like some company?"

He grinned and not just about her offer, but because he realized that she was standing beside a sprig of mistletoe. He got momentarily distracted—if he moved her over a foot he'd have the green light to kiss her—but he wasn't planning on their first kiss being a public event so he controlled his impulses. "You certain you're up for that? It's going to be a long night."

"Ha, funny man. I'm up for it. I love it when new babies are being born." She glanced down the street at the milling crowds that filled the lighted buildings and blocked off the road between the buildings. She nodded toward the gathering. "Maybe we need to go ahead and leave. Now that I know what's going on I'm worried about the mare."

He was not going to gripe about leaving early and missing another interrogation by Esther Mae and Norma Sue. "I think that's a good idea."

"Good. Because to tell you the truth dodging

mistletoe is exhausting."

He laughed. "And here I thought you hadn't noticed it."

"Are you kidding me? It's everywhere. Do you know it was above the coat rack–but I was careful not to walk under it when you were helping me put on my coat."

"Well gee, thanks," he drawled half teasing. What was he supposed to do? He'd been so intent on helping her put her coat on that he hadn't looked up. Knowing she'd known it was there and had stayed clear of it didn't help his current situation. She hadn't wanted to kiss him.

As he was mulling this over soft snow flakes began to fall again and squeals of delight ignited all along the street.

It hadn't snowed again since the day they'd cut down the tree. He flipped the collar of his sheepskin jacket up and tugged his hat a little snugger to give himself a moment more to digest the mistletoe situation. He was going to kiss Mia.

They may have always only been friends but he was about to test that theory. The positive repercussions were worth the risk. He loved her and had for a long time.

"You know what, I'd like to see the nativity scene before we leave."

She smiled. "Are you sure?"

"I'm sure, if we hurry."

"Okay then, let's go. I would love that."

They walked down the street to the live nativity scene. Three cowboys with guitars stood to the side of the rustic manger scene singing *Away in a Manger*. Many of the people were singing along with them.

Mia leaned in close. "I see they replaced the live baby with a doll. They said if the temperature dropped too low they were going to do that. It's certainly dropped."

"I was wondering about that." He looked down at her. "How are you doing?"

She tilted her face up at him and her cheeks were a pretty pink but she looked happy. "I'm fine. I wore a heavier coat tonight than the other day."

He was so tempted to brush his lips across hers, to wrap his arm around her and pull her close. "Good," he said, his voice was gruff.

"*Yoo-hoo!*" Esther Mae aka Mrs. Mistletoe hollered from the hot chocolate table. Norma Sue was grinning and Adela had joined her two friends to pass out warm beverages to the crowd. They were all smiling like kids who knew a secret.

"Y'all come on over here for some hot chocolate," Norma Sue demanded. "It'll warm your soul and tickle your heart."

Ty was a little wary of the grinning trio but he'd set himself up for this by coming down here.

Mia grinned. "You mean, grab and run. Times a ticking."

"Yes it is."

"Y'all look like you're enjoying this chilly evening?" Esther Mae cooed when they reached the table.

"Sure do," Norma Sue agreed and held up a bag of marshmallows. "How about some marshmallows to roast on the fire?"

Adela filled cups with steaming chocolate and handed the cups over to them. "This will warm you up," the dainty woman said with a smile.

"Thanks." Ty accepted the cups then handed one to Mia. Their cold fingers brushed and warmth radiated through him despite the chill of her fingertips. "I think we'll pass on the marshmallows. We have a mare at my place to check on so we'll be leaving in a moment."

All three ladies looked jubilant.

"Mia's going to help you?" Delight radiated in Esther Mae's voice.

"I am," Mia said. "I love seeing new foals." She seemed oblivious to the rapt excitement on the three ladies expressions. Esther Mae was about to burst into applause at any moment.

"I'm the same way," Norma Sue agreed. "Me and my Roy Don have helped countless foals come into this world together and I never grow tired of seeing that new baby wobble to its feet and take its first steps."

"It's a wonderful thing to share together," Esther Mae added. She came around the table and leaned close for Ty's ears only. "Here, just in case you need a little help." She slipped something in his pocket then looked from him to Mia. "You're not spending Christmas day alone are you?"

"No, ma'am. I'm going over to the ranch to have lunch with Ty and his partners."

"Oh wonderful, that will be perfect."

Pretty perfect to him, Ty agreed then led Mia away. A few minutes later they loaded up and headed toward the ranch. Mia was following him in her truck as he led the way. She'd been the one who suggested she come along.

It was going to be a great night.

CHAPTER NINE

Mia was filled with anticipation as she eased out of the truck. The stars were shining like bright jewels in the dark sky and as they'd driven away from town big snowflakes began to fall. In this area of Texas snow was a true treat. Snow that stuck to the ground and wasn't wet mush was even more of a treat. As she eased out of the truck, being careful with her knee, a thrill raced through her seeing how the snow dusted the landscape in a white coating. And it was still falling.

She held her palms out to catch a few snowflakes and smiled from the inside out. "It's beautiful."

Ty smiled too as he strode toward her. "You look like a snow globe Christmas angel standing there. And yes, it's beautiful. So are you."

Her heart raced at his compliment and the look in his eyes.

Ty was a gorgeous man. That lean face with those expressive eyes and a smile that caused tingles of attraction to ignite throughout her. Danger signals clanged through her as a sigh escaped her lips… "I love snow globes. Tonight's Christmas festivities in town would have made a sweet scene."

"Yes, it would have. Come on, Miss Snow Globe, lets go check on Velvet."

"I'd love to. I'm so excited." To her surprise he draped a casual arm across her shoulders and walked with her toward the stable. It was everything she could do not to wrap her arms around him and breathe in the scent of him.

She had it bad. So bad.

They entered the stable and soft nickers from the horses welcomed them as Ty led the way down the center of the building to a stall where a gorgeous black mare rested in the soft hay.

"*Oh.*" She halted and her hand went to her heart. "Oh, Ty, she's gorgeous, and it looks like we got here just in time."

She was having a hard time keeping her eyes off of Ty. He was so perfect here. "I'll check her out to make certain." He opened the stall and zeroed in on the mare. "Hey there, Velvet. You're doing good, pretty girl. Real good," he murmured soothingly to the soon-to-be-mama. The mare nickered and raised her head to look at Ty as he knelt. It was as if they connected in that look and the mama relaxed, at ease now that he was there.

Mia loved the way the horse trusted Ty and she completely understood the feeling.

After he finished assessing the situation he got to his feet and came out to where Mia waited. "I think everything looks good. We'll wait out here unless she starts to fret too much."

"Sounds good. I'm so glad she's doing so well."

"Me too."

He closed the stall's gate with a soft click of the metal latch and then led the way to the bench sitting on the far wall about ten feet across from Velvet's stall. "We can sit here and still see Velvet, but give her some space too."

"Perfect spot." Mia glanced back over her shoulder, afraid to turn her back for a moment in case she'd miss out.

Excitement bubbled inside of her as she sat down on the bench. It was so small their shoulders touched—Mia was a fan of whoever had picked the bench. Not only did her shoulder touch Ty's but also it was such a tight squeeze they were hip to hip. Mia willed her erratic heartbeat to calm down, which was an impossibility. Hands clasped in her lap she leaned back and tried relaxing beside Ty, who seemed as tense as she felt.

"Have you heard from your uncle?"

"I did. And, oh, Ty, he sounded so happy. It really startled me, I mean, he has always been so quiet and reserved, you know how he is. But something is different about him. He's animated and that's really, really cool."

Ty chuckled. "Love will do that, I think. Seems to have done similar magic on my partners who've all found love this year. All but Dalton that is."

"I guess," she chuckled. "They got married in Vegas and spent the night then headed straight to

Earline's place. He called me from there." It hit Mia then that he hadn't included himself in either camp of the falling in love or not in the discussion about his partners.

"He sounds like maybe his new wife is good for him."

"It does." She turned to face him. "Ty, do you think he stayed single all these years just because of me?" The idea caused a tightening in her chest.

"Only Huey would know that. Is it bothering you?"

She nodded. "Yes. He sounded so very happy and when I look back on his quietness I wonder...."

"Stop wondering. He just got married—he's *supposed* to be happy and you're supposed to be happy for him. I can tell you when the woman of my dreams says yes to my proposal and marries me—honey, I'll rope the moon with my happiness."

Mia's stomach dropped at the sincerity in his words and the way his gaze captured her. Her heart revved up and charged inside her chest. Her mouth went dry. All she could do was nod as she imagined herself as that woman. *Yes, please.*

Oh yes.

She tried to concentrate on the conversation. "I'm happy for Uncle Huey," she managed to whisper.

Ty held her gaze with his and then lifted his hand and gently traced the curve of her face with his fingertips. A shiver of awareness and longing tingled through her like love tap dancing to her heart. He let his hand drift to cup her neck and...her breath quickened...he was going to kiss her.

Velvet chose that moment to groan–signaling it was time.

Mia jumped, startled and regret lit Ty's gaze momentarily before he moved to assist the birth of the foal.

Mia could hardly breathe and it was a moment before she could move. She gathered her senses like a blanket then willed her legs to carry her to the stall. But even then it was a while before her heart found any kind of regularity once more.

Focus, cowboy. Ty warned himself as he concentrated on Velvet and her needs while he tried to get his emotions under control. The vulnerable look in Mia's eyes he'd just seen as she worried about her uncle shook him. Mia had lost her parents at a young age and he'd realized after he'd started helping her learn to ride way back then, that was a part of her that she held back from everyone.

As if she was afraid she might be hurt if she let anyone too close.

Now that he thought about it he suspected that might be part of everything she did...and probably was part of the reason she'd never won that championship. There was a part of her that was afraid to lose control and give it her all. But he was afraid too.

Ty gave Velvet a gentle rub down and then came out of the stall to stand beside Mia. "It won't be long now."

As if the mare had been waiting for him to give the go ahead she nickered and then the process began. He went back to the mare and helped where he could, mostly giving encouragement to Velvet because she had the birth under control.

And Mia beamed from the stall opening when the colt was finally born.

Ty moved out of the stall to stand beside Mia once more and over the next hour they watched as Velvet took care of her newborn colt. Mia looked in awe and near tears as they watched the little fella take his first wobbly steps.

"Oh look at him, he's so strong." Her gaze met Ty's and her smile was like sunshine. "I'm so glad you invited me to be a part of this. I could get used to it."

I could get used to you being here. Ty's heart swelled and he smiled back, not trusting himself to say anything for a minute.

She watched the colt again. "It reminds me of a time I spent in the barn with my dad as he helped a mare give birth. It's one of my favorite memories of him."

"You never forget something like that. I helped my dad deliver a few foals too. I remember every one of those. I'm glad you have that memory with your dad," he said gently.

She nodded. "It's a good one."

When they emerged from the barn it was well past midnight the snow had coated everything in white and still drifted down around them in a soft fine dusting.

Mia laughed in delight. "This has been the most amazing night and this is gorgeous."

Snow settled over her as if she were being coated in powdered sugar and he couldn't take his eyes off of her.

"It has been." He reached for her right hand and stepped toward her, gently he slipped his other hand around her waist, resting at the small of her back. She stared up at him with an expression of uncertainty on her beautiful face but then, while his heart hammered in his chest her free hand came to rest on his shoulder. "The only thing I think could make it better is a slow dance in the snow with you." He began swaying slowly with her in his arms being careful of her injured knee as he did so.

Her breath caught and her fingers tightened on

his shoulder. Their eyes held and then her gaze drifted to his lips and every cell in his body ached for her.

"Ty," she whispered.

He swallowed hard. "Is this corny?" he asked, his voice gruff. For him it was far from corny but it was all he could come up with. He'd dreamed of holding her close for so long.

She shook her head. "Oh no. I love it."

"Good. Because I love…it too." His heart raced as she rested her head against his shoulder and they continued to move to the sound of music that only they could hear.

You almost told her you loved her.

Almost kissed her.

The question was why hadn't he shared his heart with her? Why hadn't he kissed her?

CHAPTER TEN

Mia couldn't believe she was in Ty's arms and they were dancing–yes *dancing,* in the snow. She couldn't help herself, she had to take advantage of this moment and enjoy it, she laid her head against his chest and held on. His heart thundered against her cheek and suddenly she wondered…was he as nervous as she was?

She lifted her head to stare at him in wonder. He stilled and gazed deeply into her eyes and then lowered his head…he was going to kiss her.

Instead, he stopped moving. Froze. Then he blinked hard and stepped away from her. "I think it's time to get you home."

Mia was stunned. She'd wanted his kiss. Wanted it more than anything. "Um yeah, right. It's cold." And it was.

Why hadn't he kissed her?

She turned to her truck, but he beat her to it, reaching around her to open the door. She slipped into the icy chill trapped inside the closed cab of the truck. Her heart felt that way at the moment. Had they just been wrapped up in the moment and he'd almost kissed her because of that…then realized what he was doing?

"I'll follow you home to make sure you get there safely." He said as she cranked the engine.

"No, I'm fine you don't need to follow me."

"Yes, I do. It's really late and I'm not letting you drive home without knowing you made it okay."

She'd just almost made a fool of herself because he had to know by the look on her face that she'd known he was about to kiss her and that she wanted it. And now he was telling her she didn't have what it took to make it home.

"Ty, I drive dark roads by myself all the time. It's nothing."

"It is to me. I'll follow you."

"*No!* I can do it on my own."

He heaved in an exasperated breath. "There's no need to be mad—"

Her cheeks burned at that. "Mad. About what?" She glared at him as her embarrassment over the near kiss turned to anger.

His jaw tensed but he didn't speak at first. "Drive, Mia. I'm following you and there's nothing you can do to stop me."

He closed the door and strode toward his truck. She wanted him. The whole package. To have and to hold and to be hers till the end of time. "Lot of good that's doing you," she muttered then drove toward the ranch exit.

Despite her objections Ty followed at a distance and when she reached her house he stayed inside his truck as she got out and let herself into the house. She didn't acknowledge him being there. She just unlocked the door and slipped inside. Then she slumped against the door and listened to him leave.

What a mess she was in.

She moved to the pale blue couch that had been in the room since before her parents were killed in the car wreck. Feeling suddenly drained she sank down onto it. Her mind whirled replaying the magic moments of the night. Everything about the night had been wonderful. Up until the moment he'd decided not to kiss her.

Reaching down she removed the brace from her knee and moved it. The pain was getting better and the doctor had told her it would be okay to remove the brace after two weeks—if she was having no pain. She'd still be required to limit her activities and take it easy on the knee but that in time it would be back to normal.

She'd feared at first that it was career ending. And that had surprised her how much she hadn't minded that prognosis.

Looking around the room that had once been shared by her and her parents, she felt comfort there...for the first time since losing them.

There were photos of her dad at the NFR competing five years in a row. His dream for as long as she was able to remember had been to win the National Finals Rodeo championship in calf roping. That had been his focus and her earliest memories of him were watching through the slats of the arena as he sat on his horse and roped calves over and over again.

Later she remembered her and her mom traveling with him but then as she'd gotten older and was in school, her mom stayed home and he was gone on the road a lot. The night they'd died Mia had stayed the weekend with a friend while her mother went with him to a rodeo in Colorado. It was the first time her mother had gone in a long time.

Mia rubbed her knee, lost in the memories. She never saw her parents again.

And she'd felt lost for so long.

Until she'd decided to go after her father's dream—Mia halted on that thought. Her father's dream.

Shouldn't she have thought her dream?

She let the thought brew... Had she been chasing a dream of being a champion because her daddy had died before he could achieve his dream?

Was that a crazy idea?

The day before her mother and dad started the

cross country trip to that last rodeo Mia had asked her mother why she didn't go more often. And her mother had smiled that sweet smile Mia always loved, she'd touched Mia's face so tenderly and Mia could still hear her words.

"Honey, the rodeo is your dad's dream. My dream, aside from being his wife was you. I wanted to be a wife and mother all my life and I don't want to miss out on one minute with you. So for now, I'm very content to stay home and be your mother and let your dad reach for the rest of his dream."

Mia got up from the couch and moved carefully toward her bedroom. She had some changes to make in her life.

And they needed to be her changes.

She smiled. And for the first time in a very long time a pressure inside of her eased.

"Man, what are you doing?"

A rooster crowed from somewhere on the property as Ty pulled up on the reins of the cutting horse he was working. He spun the horse around in a tight circle so he was looking at the arena fence where Dalton and Rafe stood watching him. It had been two days since he'd danced with Mia in the falling snow. Two days since he'd almost kissed her and told her he loved her.

And each of those days he'd risen extra early and gone to bed late. He'd worked with the horses he had in the stable and added hours on by working with Sinbad. He'd worked until he was bone weary and mind numb...or at least he'd tried for that.

Rafe hung his elbows over the rungs of the arena. "I know cowboys are supposed to be known for working from sunup to sundown, but, buddy, don't you think you're taking it a tad too far?"

"All I got ta say, buddy..." Dalton drawled with a grin. "...is if you keep this up and stop getting your beauty sleep the lady is certainly going to have a problem with the packaging."

Rafe laughed. "He's got a point. You look rough. What's got you so tied up in knots?"

Ty scowled at them. They were his partners but also his friends and they knew him better than most. That meant they knew that when he had something on his mind he processed it best from the back of a horse. Ty had always been more comfortable with horses than with people. The only problem was that his stomach was as tied in knots today as it had been the night he'd watched Mia enter her home and close the door without looking back at him.

"I have some things on my mind."

"You mean a woman," Dalton challenged again.

"You aren't going to let this go are you?"

Dalton chuckled. "Well, no, I am not. You are a man in love and any fool can see it."

"I've gotta say that's what it appears to be," Rafe agreed. "Kind of gets you in the gut and won't let go. Keeps you awake thinking about it. And it will keep doing that until you give into it."

Ty loped the horse from the center of the pen to the fence. "Okay, yeah, I'm in love. Have been for years but a lot of good it's done me. She's back and she'll be leaving again soon. I can't stand in the way of that. Never could."

Rafe's brows dipped and he met him with challenge. "You won't know until you talk to her. Have you told her?"

"No, I almost did...but I couldn't do it."

"Is that because you're scared?" Dalton grunted. "You're not scared of anything. I've seen you working with horses that just as soon run you over and kick your skull in. You're fearless, bud."

"It's different," Rafe said with understanding. "Let me just tell you that if you don't tell her how you feel you're doing her and you an injustice. She has a right to know. She has a right to choose the path she wants."

Dalton nodded. "Absolutely. And who says she can't love you and still make her dreams come true. Lots of cowboys and cowgirls rodeo full-time and marry too."

Ty knew what the problem was, Mia had had opportunities over the last four years to come home and she'd seldom done it. When she did come it was a quick sweep into town and out again within a day or two without seeing anyone else. She was like a ghost or something. He assumed that in between those times she spent a lot of time living in small quarters of her horse trailer, which were nice but had to get old after four years. Either that or she was staying somewhere else when she had any time off. And that was what worried him. Fact was, she didn't want to come home.

If that was so then he didn't stand a chance.

"She's had opportunities to come home and she didn't. Do you seriously think she's going to stay here when it's obvious she's not happy here?

Dalton and Rafe looked at each other then back at him and he could see this was something they hadn't thought about.

It was Dalton who spoke first. "Seems to me you're asking the wrong people. Come on Ty, take a risk and talk to her."

"Really talk to her," Rafe challenged.

They left him after that, heading out to work cattle before the brewing storm blew in. He kept working his horses needing every moment he could get.

Christmas was coming and the "do-over" that he'd so fancifully dreamed about had turned out to

129

be just a dream to him. The reality was that he lived in the real world and the reality was that Mia ever wanting to stay in this little town, even for short periods of time, had never seemed to be anything she was interested in.

So the reality was, why had he even for a minute thought he stood a chance with her?

CHAPTER ELEVEN

Mia had hidden out at home for another two days instead of going to Ty's and checking on his progress with Sinbad. She had things on her mind, him included, and he didn't need her telling him how to handle the horse.

She decorated her tree with ornaments from the attic–it had been tricky getting up the stairs with a brace on but she'd managed it. She'd found the boxes of ornaments her mother had stored there many years ago. It took most of the day, but by afternoon she had it done. She'd needed the time to reconnect with her mother. To feel something more inside this house than sad memories of loss. She'd taken each ornament out of the tissue paper it had been wrapped in and she'd remembered a sweet, happy time she'd shared with her mother as they'd decorated the tree. And by the time she'd finished, she'd shed a few tears...a lot of tears. But she'd smiled too. And through it all that was what she clung to.

This house, this home was more than the keeper of what she'd once had and would never have again. It was the place she'd once been happy. She'd forgotten that part.

The sky outside her window was darkening ominously when she finally turned the tree lights on that second day of holing up alone with her memories and thoughts. Joy, not sadness filled her as she watched them twinkle.

Smiling and with a heart full of emotion she called Uncle Huey. She just needed to hear his voice. Needed to hear the voice of someone she loved. Though she might not have always come home like she should have, she realized why that was now, she and Uncle Huey had always talked on a regular basis. He'd given her time. Time to heal in her own way even when she hadn't known she was healing.

He sounded happy on the other end of the line.

"Mia girl, how are you doing? I'm having a blast out here."

"I'm okay. I'm glad you're happy—"She paused, thinking she heard laughter and something squealing in the background. "Is that pigs?"

He chuckled, then laughed as if something funny was happening around him. "That's piglets and Earline laughing. We're outside trying to round up a herd of babies that escaped the pen. Earline is chasing them down." A loud yelp could be heard followed by more laughter.

"Oh, I've gotta go. Earline just landed in a mud hole and I need to rescue her." He was laughing when the phone went dead.

Mia was smiling as she set the phone on the table. Her heart felt light imagining her mild, mannered uncle chasing baby pigs around the yard and rescuing Earline from the mud. She was so happy for him.

Feeling better than she'd felt in a really long time she pulled on her coat and went to the stable to check on her horse and make sure she was set for the icy evening that was approaching.

"Hey, Jubilee. How you doin' girl? I know you're happy not being cooped up in the trailer." Jubilee nickered and nudged her with her soft nose in answer. Mia gave her a hug.

They'd lived far too many hours of the year on the road. Mia, living inside the cramped quarters of her apartment in the horse trailer and Jubilee in the back quarters. The rig was nice and one of the perks from having the trailer company as a sponsor. But in order to maintain the status she needed to keep a sponsor like them on board and for providing the gorgeous trailer, she'd needed more traveling time and appearances than she normally would. They'd helped make it possible for her to support herself through the last three years and she'd done what she needed to do to maintain their support. She hadn't had it that first year and it had been rough. What she'd been able to afford on her own was a very old trailer with living quarters for her the size of a tea bag.

"We made it okay, girlfriend," she said, giving her friend another hug and a pat on the head before she began putting fresh hay in the stall and then filled her trough with water.

Sleet was starting to come down outside as Mia emerged from the barn. The weather report had said it was only going to get worse. She was ready though. She had a nice warm fire going in the hearth and soup cooking on the stove. She could easily transfer the soup to the heavy pot that would stay warm on the hearth if the electricity went out. Cowboy cooking was one thing Uncle Huey had taught her. She could have made that soup from scratch using the fireplace as her stove if she'd needed to.

Pulling her coat tighter she dipped her chin as she moved carefully toward the back porch. Her knee was doing better and she'd left the brace off, testing it again. But she realized now this might not have been the best time for that. She certainly didn't need to slip down.

Cold, icy sleet stung her cheeks and the wind had picked up. A howl sounded somewhere in the distance. Mia halted. Was that the wind or had she really heard something howl. She turned to scan the surroundings. The howl came again and this time she knew it wasn't the wind. But the wind caused her once more not to know from which direction the sound had come.

The shed?

She took a step toward the small shed that sat at the back of the property. The barbed wire fence that separated the yard from the pastures was just behind the building. Not too far from the fence was a gully that cut through the property. Mia had always wanted to play in the gully as a child, but her parents had been very diligent in warning her away from the place. It really wasn't that deep, but it could have been dangerous for a child.

The howl came again and for a moment she thought it was coming from beneath the shed. Then she realized it wasn't. It was coming from the gully.

The sleet was worse now, and her face stung from the tiny, icy pelts that were hitting her and wetting down her hair. She should have worn her hood.

Her knee was starting to hurt as she slipped through the top two rungs of barbed wire and started toward the small ravine.

She reached the edge and looked down at the small stream that cut through the bottom of the gap twenty feet or so below her. Cow trails weaved their way down the slope creating natural paths through the underbrush. And somewhere down there the mournful cry of a dog…she was pretty certain, called to her.

She bit her lip as she contemplated the situation. The animal obviously needed help.

But could she get down the slope without hurting her knee?

And when she got down there what would she find?

Mia didn't know the answer to either of these questions. All she knew was that she had to help the animal making the sad, wailing cry for help.

"You can do this," she muttered as she navigated the slick grass, carefully placing her boot down on an area that had a little grip.

The problem, her hands. They were shaking from the cold as she used a small tree to steady herself before taking the next step downward on the incline. "There, that wasn't so hard to do—" It was the second step she didn't make.

Her foot hit a slick, muddy spot on the slope and before she could grab the tree, or even a clump of grass she was falling. And then rolling. Her hip hit the ground as she tried hard to throw her legs up rather than let her knees twist in the process.

When she came to a halt at the bottom of the gully, one booted foot was in the water along with half her body the other half was sunk into the thick mud as if she was about to make a mud angel.

She groaned, lifted her head and looked down the length of her body. No blood and guts but, she wasn't totally certain she could move. She held her head out of the mud, glad that at least seemed possible. And then she heard the growl.

Not a howl, but a menacing, angry growl...

Ty was leading the colt he'd been working back to the stable when his phone rang. Phone service in the Mule Hollow countryside was spotty at best so he wasn't surprised when the crackle of a bad connection greeted him. "Hello," he said, though with the way the line was garbled he doubted he would be able to make out who was on the other end of the line. The sleet that had started falling wasn't helping.

He thought he heard a voice so he tried again. "Hello, you're not coming through."

"Ty...hel-...mud...growling, help—" Ty struggled to make out even the little he understood as he focused on "help" the one word from a familiar voice that he'd know anywhere.

"Mia, do you need help?"

"Y..." the line went dead.

Instantly, Ty was moving toward the stall. He let the horse inside then jogged down the center of the stable and out into the falling sleet. He yanked open his truck door, jumped in and had it cranked in a half a second and heading down the lane. He drove as fast as he dared on the ice slickened roads, knowing that he needed to get there fast but that landing in a ditch and having to dig himself out would only cost him time in the long run.

Instead, he drove fast but safe as he made the ten mile drive to her small ranch.

His adrenaline was in overdrive as he brought the truck to a skidding halt and then jumped from the cab and jogged up the slick steps. Knocking on the door he wasn't surprised to see that she wasn't inside. Or if she was something was wrong. Just in case that was the problem he twisted the door handle and when it swung open he stepped into the house. A warm fire welcomed him in the fireplace and the scent of something warm and delicious filled the air. "Mia. Where are you?" He called but received no answer. He tried to hold the panic down that was clawing at him. She was a capable woman who'd been living on her own, fending for herself for several years now–she was okay.

But no matter how many times he'd tried to reassure himself the garbled message worried him. Outside again, he headed toward the barn. The sleet was stronger now and the severe weather warning that had swept in had worsened in the last fifteen minutes.

Everything in the barn seemed fine. Mia's rodeo horse munched fresh hay in its stall. It looked as if Mia had taken care of the horse not long ago. So that was a good sign.

He strode outside into the sleet again. "*Mia,*" he yelled into the wind as he studied the landscape. Then he saw the very faint tracks on the ground. He saw them coming into the barn and going out. He followed them, grateful the slushy sleet hadn't covered them up completely. He stood where there was a marking…as if she'd stood there and then turned. He crouched down and studied the markings harder. And then he saw another track. It was heading toward the shed. He stood and scanned that area and sure enough he could just make out a very few faint tracks.

"Mia," he yelled again. And kept yelling as he jogged to the shed. He yanked open the door but there was only garden tools. He shut the door and walked around the small building and then he saw the track beside the fence.

"Mia," he yelled again, and slipped between the barbed wire to the other side as his insides twisted.

141

A faint sound rode the wind.

He called her name again and started jogging toward the trees making out a boot print every few feet.

"*Ty.*"

He heard his name as he reached the edge of the gully and scanned the muddy, steep slope. There, he spotted her laying near the small stream.

Relief and worry intertwined as he started down the steep slope. He thanked the Lord for answering his prayers as he went. He was almost to her when he heard the growl and saw her lift her hand in a palm out, halting motion. He slid on the incline grabbing a tree to stop himself as he saw, not a look of pain on her face but of warning. She was covered in mud but there was a small smile playing across her lips. He was certain he also saw pain in her eyes. She pointed and through the icy rain he saw a dog. It was soaked and hard to make out much except the snarling teeth that were exposed as it watched him warily. And beside it, he thought he saw movement...puppies? Yup. Tiny, very newborn puppies that weren't going to make it too long in this weather.

"I can't move…very well," Mia said, her voice hoarse. "Knee's tweaked a bit."

"You hold tight. I'll get you out of there and then I'll worry about the little family you've found." He moved cautiously down the path, moving so that he made a wider arch and came in from Mia's feet rather than her head. Hoping if he could come in from as far away from the scared mama pooch that she might keep her distance and continue to warn them away without choosing to attack. If she did attack he'd throw himself between it and Mia, but at the moment there was no reason to not be cautious.

He reached her, and placed his hand on her boot. "So, can I lift you?" he asked keeping one eye on the dog.

"Yes, I might yelp, but maybe not. I'm just warning you in case I wimp out on you. L-lift me anyway. Laying here in the mud i-isn't doing me or my knee any good. I can't believe I did this."

Hearing her teeth chattering had him wanting to hurry but he needed to move with caution.

"Where's your brace?" He just noticed it was missing.

"At…house." She closed her eyes.

Ty could see pale blue tinging her skin. He had to get her out of here. Scooting slowly up beside her he placed his back to the scared dog then slipped his arms beneath Mia. She opened her eyes and met his. She was shivering. "Ready?"

She gave a weak nod. "Ready."

"Here we go." He lifted her and stood in one movement, thankfully the dog chose only to growl. "Good, mama," Ty said, soothingly to the dog. "Keep watch on those babies and I'll be back."

Mia rested her head against his shoulder and nodded. He wasn't sure her not grunting or crying out was a good sign or a bad sign. She was shivering uncontrollably as he held her close and started up the hill.

Unable to get through the fence once he made the long rough hike up the slippery slope he walked down the fence line until he reached the gate. It took him a few minutes longer but he didn't have to put Mia down as he unhooked the chain holding the gate closed and that was good. He didn't see any cattle around so he didn't bother closing it again. He'd come back later and close it. Right now he was only worried about getting Mia inside the house.

"How are you doing?" he asked as they crossed the sleet slickened yard.

"I've been...better," she said, stuttering some but with a smile in her voice even as cold as she was. "But...I could be a whole lot worse."

"I'm just glad I got your call." He didn't want to think about what might have happened if she hadn't been able to get hold of him or someone. He was thankful she'd had her phone with her and been conscious and able to use it.

She looked up at him and gave a weary, brave smile. "I am too."

CHAPTER TWELVE

"Heat. Now we're talking," Ty said as he carried her through the back door into the kitchen. "When you get out of those cold, wet clothes you'll feel better."

Sleet clung to both of them. Mia had been concentrating hard to control the shivers as Ty carried her up the hill and home. Now that they were inside and she felt the warmth from both the furnace and the fireplace she was more than a little grateful.

In the time it took for the poor man to come to her rescue—a rescue she'd thankfully been coherent enough to remember. She'd felt his concern as he'd reached her and had completely appreciated him as he'd carried her out of the gully.

She was so cold at the moment that it was hard

to appreciate anything but the warmth of the kitchen. There was the pain in her knee but she'd pretty much tuned it out with the numbness from the cold.

"Can you sit in a chair? We need–you need, to get out of those clothes." "I can sit there, in the kitchen chair." She was shivering almost uncontrollably and understood the need to get the wet coat off and the clothes.

He pulled the chair out with his boot then carefully set her down. Every muscle hurt and she had a feeling she was in for a few rough days, however, she didn't feel like she'd hurt anything other than her knee and her pride.

"My, robe is hanging on a hook in my closet. First r-room on the right up the stairs."

He didn't hesitate as he left the room and she could hear him taking the stairs and making quick work of it. She started trying to unzip the jacket but her hands were shaking too much. And there was mud everywhere.

He returned with her fuzzy red robe in his hand. "Here, let me help with that," he said, laying the robe on the table, he then knelt in front of her and unzipped the jacket. His beautiful eyes were grave with concern. "You're a mess but I'm not exactly sure how to work this." He tugged on the sleeve and pulled the sloppy, muddy wet jacket from one arm and then helped peel it from the other. Then he removed her boots and socks.

She appreciated his concern for her modesty but she was in a pickle. "I can get the shirt off by myself, but these soaked jeans are going to be tough."

"You get that shirt off and slip that robe on and we'll get those pants off."

She had to fight the smile that his determination caused in her. If she hadn't been so stinking cold she might have laughed. He left the room and she managed to get the shirt unbuttoned and off. Most of the mud went with the coat and there wasn't much left under the shirt. Just cold damp skin. She tugged her robe on and then stood, keeping her weight on her good leg. Her legs were weak and shaking but she managed to wrestle the soaked jeans down around her thighs before sinking back to the chair. She called Ty back into the room. "Sorry, this is all I could manage."

One day they'd laugh at this…but not right now.

"Okay," he knelt down and met her gaze with shadowed eyes. "You hold onto your robe and I'll peel these things off and chunk them in the wash room."

She did just what he said and was relieved after he was able to literally peel them off and drop them at her feet. He left the room and returned in a moment with two towels. He handed her one and she used it to pat her legs dry.

"Let me wrap your muddy hair in this towel then I'll carry you to the living room where the fire is. We need to get you warmed up now that the wet gear is gone."

Within moments he had the towel around her head and he'd lifted her into his arms again. This time she was fully aware of every tense muscle as he carried her into the living room. The lights were on and the fire was crackling in the fireplace as he eased her onto the couch. There was a throw blanket draped over the back of the couch and he tugged it down and around her. Then he fluffed the pillows.

"Are you feeling warmer?"

She nodded. "Better."

He placed a hand to her neck and felt her skin and her insides warmed at his touch. She was definitely starting to come out of the chilled state.

"Is that soup I smell?"

"Yes."

"I'll be right back."

He left the room and she leaned her head back on the pillows and snuggled deeper beneath the blanket. She hurt all over but her knee miraculously didn't seem to be as bad as she'd feared. She just felt tired. And her mind was overrun with thoughts of Ty.

"Here you go, this will help warm you up."

She opened her eyes and found him sitting on the edge of the coffee table again, holding out a bowl of steaming soup.

"Did you know you were going to have an accident and need this soup? That's pretty intuitive."

She chuckled and sat back up. "Thank you, and no, I'm not that good. I just knew with the ice storm coming that hot soup was the perfect thing to have in case the electricity went out and I found myself camping by the fire."

"That works too." He handed her the warm bowl and the heat instantly radiated from the bowl through her chilled hands. When he cupped his hands over hers as she took it from him butterflies filled her.

Oh how she could get used to having this man around. If only…

"If you're okay, I'll go out and see if I can help that mother dog and her pups. I'm afraid it might be too late, but I can't just leave them out there."

Her heart warmed more. "Thank you so much. I don't know how you'll manage. Poor thing she was being so protective of them despite being exposed to the elements and so cold. She might attack you."

"I'll manage. You stay put and I'll be back shortly."

She watched him go. Certain that if anyone could help the little mother it would be him. Maybe he was a dog whisperer too. The thought made her smile. He could whisper to her any day.

She took her first bite of the soup and let the warmth slide down through her. This was exactly what she needed while she waited on Ty to return.

The heat helped knock the arctic freeze from her brain and slowly but surely she began to feel human again. By the time Ty returned at least an hour later she was feeling more like herself. He on the other hand was soaked but as far as she could tell he didn't appear to have any dog bites.

And that was a plus.

"Did you rescue them? Are they still alive?"

He removed his hat and set it on the hearth then pulled off the wet coat. He was dry underneath it and his jeans weren't too wet. She was glad, he'd warm up quicker this way. He ran a hand through his dark hair.

She held her breath waiting for his answer.

"They made it," he said at last and she breathed a sigh of relief. "They're in the barn snuggled up in the corner in a warm bundle of fresh dry hay. The mother was past the fighting stage when I got back. I took a blanket and a bucket I found in the barn. And some lunchmeat I found in the fridge. I'll get her some dog food in the morning. But that did the trick for now. She was so busy eating that it gave me time to load the five babies into the bucket and carry them up the hill."

"That sounds almost too easy."

"Tell me about it. I went down there prepared to be eaten alive to save those puppies and the mom too. You must have been saying some powerful prayers."

She laughed. "I was praying alright."

"Then there you go. That's all I can explain it with, because *that* little mama was out to *eat* me for lunch earlier."

Mia chuckled then her smile faded as their gazes held. "Ty." She scooted over on the couch and patted the cushion. "You've been my hero today. Truly. I need to talk."

He sat down and took her hands. "Mia—"

"No. Please. I need to say something," she

interrupted.

"Okay."

She took a fortifying breath. "When I was twelve I lost the mother I loved, who'd always been there for me. And I lost my father, the man I loved and idolized…sometimes from afar because he was gone so much. It devastated me." She blinked hard to hold back the tears and to be able to finish. "I was blessed that Uncle Huey came here to live, to carry on where my parents left off…but I couldn't wait to run from here. I could only relate this house to what I'd had. And I closed my heart up because I couldn't stand the idea of losing anyone ever again. And that included Uncle Huey. Yes, I loved him but, I closed off part of myself from him and everyone. Being on the road, chasing…my dad's dream kept me busy, away from here. But lonely."

Ty's hands tightened on hers. He didn't say anything though, just gave her the support to go on. It was so Ty, and she loved him to the moon and back.

"You helped me become good on my horse.

You helped me learn what it meant to have a good friend. And what you don't know is that you found a way into my heart when I wouldn't let anyone else in." She blinked hard. "And you sent me away to pursue my dreams."

"Mia, I let you go because–I couldn't stand in the way of you reaching for your dreams."

"The only problem is, that I've finally realized something. I left here not chasing my dream but my dad's dreams. It was a way to be close to him. A way to give him his championship. It had meant so much to him that he was gone three out of four weekends a month many times seeking it. I've been chasing my dad's dreams while I was running from mine."

His brows dipped and his hand went slack on hers. "What?"

She managed a hesitant smile. "My dream was the thing I feared the most. It's the same dream that my mother always had but I've been running from it. Because to have that dream it meant risking my heart. Risking loving someone and losing them. It meant telling you I-I love you and knowing that opens me up for rejection and loss."

Mia could hardly breathe as she got the words out and saw the look in Ty's eyes shadow. He tensed then he stood up...and turned his back on her.

CHAPTER THIRTEEN

Ty's heart was about to beat out of his chest as he came to his feet and spun to stare into the fire while he tried to process what Mia was telling him. She loved him.

Had loved him.

And he hadn't known it.

He closed his eyes and let the knowledge sink in. He spun back toward her then sat back down. "Mia, I let you go because…because I loved you so much. And I wanted you to have your dreams. I had no idea you loved me."

"Oh, Ty," she gasped. "I hoped…when I was laying down there in the gully all I could think about was that I hadn't ever told you the truth. I had no idea you felt this way too."

Unable to help himself any longer Ty cupped

her face with his hands and kissed her. Fire and emotion intertwined instantly igniting through him. But he drew back, still unable to believe they were finally talking. Finally, letting their hidden feelings free.

"I can't believe I never knew," he said.

She traced the line of his face with her fingers, they left a fire trailing behind them. Her eyes teared up and she blinked several times. "I have loved you for so long. But couldn't admit it. Because I was running from the truth. Ty, I'm not going back to the circuit. I'm retiring as of now. I'll figure out something to do here to support myself but I'm done with chasing my father's dream. I'm coming home."

"But, you've wanted that for so long—"

She shook her head. "It may have seemed that way but like I said earlier…I realized I was really running from what I really wanted." She smiled a sad little smile that hurt his heart for her. "When I was a girl my mother told me that she was content to stay home while my dad chased his dream every weekend because that was his dream. And that he'd given her her dream and that was home and family. Me. And that when he got to be there it was our perfect time as a family, but she was content to let him reach for his dream because it fulfilled him. And that I along with him fulfilled her. Ty, my real dream is to be a mother and a wife and to have a family. I hate being on the road. I hate it with a passion. I was just afraid of my real dream because it meant opening my heart to the possibility of losing the ones I loved."

He took her hands in his. "But the risk is worth the reward."

She nodded. "I realize that now. I would never take back loving my parents. Never."

Ty slid from the couch to his knee. His heart felt like it would burst. "Mia Shaw, you've been my dream and my prayer for as long as I've known you and before that it was the dream of you. I want...I love you. I want to cherish you, to grow old with you. To laugh with you. To love you...to have children with you. Will you marry me?"

Tears that had been threatening all evening spilled from her sweet eyes. "Oh, Ty. I thought you'd never ask. Yes. Oh yes."

He wrapped his arms around her and kissed her with all of his heart.

"This is going to be the perfect Christmas," he said after a long while.

"And why do you say that," she chuckled as she kissed him again.

He smiled at her. "Because this year I got my Christmas wish. I got you."

And then he kissed her again…and again.

And again…

EPILOGUE

Christmas day sparkled with the snow that had fallen on Christmas Eve. Mia and Ty had joined their friends for Christmas Eve at the Cowboy Church on the outskirts of town for a candlelight service. The snow hadn't started falling as they'd gathered outside under a star sprinkled sky but it was on the forecast. They'd sung Silent Night beneath the stars and then the pastor, wearing his cowboy hat and sheepskin coat, had read the story of Jesus' birth to the crowd.

Ty had wrapped an arm around Mia and held her close as they'd shared the special evening. Mia's heart filled with so much emotion that she'd had a hard time processing it all. So many wonderful things had happened over her short time home. She thanked God for bringing her home and for the many blessings she felt. The gentle snow had begun to fall as the pastor finished but no one made a move to leave. They'd stayed and sang more songs. Celebrating the birth of Christ was, after all, the reason for Christmas.

Now, standing in the large living room of the New Horizon Ranch's big house, Mia admired the gorgeous tree with its sparkling lights that signified new life...today it meant so much to her because she felt like she was starting a new life.

Here, with all of her new friends surrounding her, Mia felt so blessed and so very excited about what the future held for her...and Ty.

Laughter and conversations abounded and as they all gathered together for lunch. They sat around the giant table in the dining room and shared a turkey and dressing dinner that she, Sadie, Amber, and Maddie had cooked together. There was a lot of teasing from the guys about the crispy edges of the turkey, but it was all in good fun. From what Ty told her none of the ladies were particularly adept in the kitchen, but then neither were the guys. They were happy though and that was what counted.

Mia fit right into the group as being on the road so much had meant she did far more eating out than any human ought to have to do. She was excited about doing simple things like learning to cook. And she'd loved joining in on the fun of the morning as all of them had gathered in the kitchen to prepare this meal.

After lunch was over, Ty led her into to the Christmas tree and took her hands in his so they faced each other. His expression was so loving Mia's heart began hammering in her chest. Oh how she loved this man.

"Mia," he said, his voice gentle as he reached into his pocket and pulled out a small box. "I want to make this official."

Mia gasped, her pulse skipped a few beats and joy filled her despite the tears that slipped from her eyes.

"I love you, Mia and I'm not trying to rush you. I just couldn't wait to make our engagement official. I want to tell the world—do you like it. We can take it back-"

"I love it." Mia interrupted him, unable to take her eyes from the emerald cut diamond engagement ring. "It's perfect." She looked up saw that the light in his eyes matched that of the stars that had been in the sky the night before.

His smile took her breath away and she watched as he took the ring from the box and placed it easily on her finger. It was a perfect fit. They both stared down at it in awe.

"A-hem," Dalton gave a fake cough as he came into the room. They both jumped and started to laugh.

Dalton leaned back into the kitchen where everyone had been hanging out around the dessert tables. "Hey, partners, looks like maybe something good is happening by the Christmas tree."

Suddenly, a herd of smiling couples pushed him into the room and surrounded Ty and Mia.

"Well," Maddie Rose said. "Anything your partners need to know, Ty Calder?"

Ty didn't let Mia go, just kept both arms around her and smiled down at her before shooting his partners and their spouses a smile.

"Mia has agreed to marry me."

Hoots and high fives erupted as everyone congratulated them. Tears of joy filled Mia's eyes, she'd found her place at last. Home, the love of her life and good friends.

She hugged Ty and snuggled in close and never planned to let go.

Dalton watched his buddy Ty looking happier than he'd ever looked in all the years Dalton had known him. All of his partners were settled and enjoying the new lives they were creating with their spouses…and now Ty would join Maddie, Rafe, and Chase in this new chapter in their lives. The next thing he knew someone would be having a baby. Whoa, that was way out of Dalton's league though and a place he never planned to go himself.

But he was happy for all of his friends. He moved forward and clapped Ty on the back. "Congratulations, you two. Though, you are hanging me out to dry as the only single partner," he grinned at Ty. "But I can hold that position down just fine all by my lonesome. I'm really glad for y'all."

"Thanks, Dalton," Ty said. "I couldn't help myself."

Mia chuckled. "Thanks for understanding." Her blue eyes crinkled at the edges. "Your time is coming."

"Oh that's okay," he assured her. "I'm not the marrying type and am content just the way I am. I'll be the single uncle to the swarm of kiddos I foresee filling up this big room in the years to come." At least he'd try to be as best he could.

Later, Dalton pulled on his jacket and went out to check on the horses for Ty. As he left the warmth of the house and entered the brisk, cold air outside he was smiling. He loved his work. He was good at it and he could give to work what was expected. He was cut out for it. A family on the other hand required things from a man that Dalton wasn't cut out for and he knew it.

Nope. He was just fine the way he was. Alone and unhitched. He had friends and that was enough.

He paused at the entrance of the stable and glanced at the ranch surrounding him. He'd set roots down here and when CC Calvert had named him as one of the beneficiaries of this amazing ranch, he'd given Dalton a reason to stick around. He'd given Dalton a place to finally hang his hat. And now that he was here, he was glad.

Dalton loved the ranch and as he stood there he felt a tinge of regret-but for the most part he was content. Life was good and a man couldn't ask for anything more than that...

Or could he... Be sure and checkout Dalton's story...he's about to find out that sometimes the best laid plans have a way of getting waylaid when turned upside down by love.

New Horizon Ranch: Mule Hollow Series

Her Mule Hollow Cowboy (Book 1)

Five ranch-hands inherit a Texas ranch from their boss. These cowboys and cowgirl vow to honor their beloved boss by making the New Horizon Ranch the success he envisioned when he chose to leave his legacy in their care. Along the way they each find the love of a lifetime. You'll fall in love with these fun, sweet, emotional love stories.

Cowboy Cliff Masterson saw a woman in need and stepped in—because Maddie was too stubborn to ask…

Cowgirl Maddie Rose has never belonged anywhere but she's just inherited part of New Horizon Ranch—along with her partners, four handsome, extremely capable cowboys… Maddie's trying to adjust to her new life and her new partners she's still unable to believe she's an owner of this fabulous ranch. Not sure why she was included, she's out to prove herself worthy of the honor of the inheritance. Loving her new life in the small Texas town of Mule Hollow, she's determined that, for the first time in her life, she's going to finally belong somewhere…

Professional Bull Rider Cliff Masterson has been chasing his dreams for years—or has he been running from his past? He's searching for more in life and ready to dig in his spurs and put down roots deep in the heart of Texas. Rescuing a beautiful cowgirl from being trampled by a bull has him dreaming of romance, home and hearth.

But Maddie's had enough people in her life leave and she's not willing to risk her heart on him— Sparks fly as he's determined to prove to the feisty cowgirl that the only think he's chasing now is wedding bells with her…

Can the Matchmakin' Posse of Mule Hollow help this couple find their happily ever after?

Rafe (Book 2)

When runaway bride, Sadie Archer's car breaks down on the outskirts of Mule Hollow, Texas, she's not exactly dressed to fix the blown tire. Then again, she hadn't planned on this road trip or her life falling apart a week before her wedding. But now that she's hit the road, destination unknown, Sadie's decided it's time to disappear for a while and find out exactly what it is she wants out of life. But first she needs to change her flat tire and that is easier said than done when one is wearing…

A bunny suit!

Ex-cowboy star Rafe Masterson thinks he's seeing things at first but yes—that is definitely a female head sticking out of the furry white bunny suit, tangling with a spare tire. A cowboy who guards his heart carefully, he's still always willing to help someone in need…even one wearing white fur from top to bottom. Completely captivated by the unusual woman, Rafe senses she's in trouble in more ways than the flat tire. He's part owner of the New Horizon Ranch and offers her a job as cook—even though they don't need a cook.

Sadie accepts even though she can't really cook but this is the perfect answer to her needs right now…and how hard can it be anyway?

These two might be down-on-love but love hasn't given up on them and the Matchmaking Posse of Mule Hollow has just gotten them in their sights...

Chase (Book 3)

Being a bridesmaid at her best friend's wedding in the sleepy town of Mule Hollow Texas is the perfect place for Amber Rivers to lay low to avoid a stalker hot on her heels back in Houston. She loves her job and her city life and isn't looking to stay long in the country-but she's blindsided by her attraction to the self-assured rancher, Chase Hartley...

Chase agrees to watch over socialite Amber while his partner heads off on his honeymoon but despite the high voltage sparks lighting up between them he has no intention of getting any closer to Amber than necessary to keep her safe. But he soon realizes there's a whole lot more to Amber than he first assumed and keeping his distance is becoming harder with every passing moment they're together.

An outside threat plus a little friendly tampering from the meddling Matchmakin' Posse of Mule Hollow puts this couple on high alert as they try not to fall in love.

Ty (Book 4)

Best friends forever…happily ever that is…Christmas wedding bells will be ringing if the Matchmakin' Posse of Mule Hollow can get this stubborn cowboy and cowgirl together under the mistletoe for the most anticipated kiss of the holiday.

Will Ty Calder, mild mannered partner in the New Horizon Ranch, get his secret Christmas wish and heal his lonesome heart this season? Find out in Book 4 of the New Horizon Ranch/Mule Hollow series.

Horse trainer Ty Calder did the right thing four years ago and sent his best friend, Mia Shaw off with a hug and best wishes in her quest for her rodeo dreams to come true. But now she's back for the Christmas holiday and he's not sure he can send her off again without revealing his true feelings…

Mia is back in Mule Hollow healing up from an injury that could end her run for the championship. But, lately her heart's not been completely committed to her rodeo dreams and Ty has her thinking he might just be the reason.

Suddenly, tensions are running high between Mia

and Ty…sparks are flying and have been spotted by the Matchmakin' Posse. Now these two are dodging mistletoe, matchmakers and the kiss they're both fighting to avoid and longing for.

But Ty can't believe Mia is ready to give up on her dreams when she's so close…he knows it means more to her than most people realize. No matter how much he wants a life with Mia he refuses to stand in the way of her dreams even if it means losing her forever…

It may take his four partners at the New Horizon Ranch and the town of Mule Hollow to get these two believing Christmas is especially the time that love can conquer all.

This is going to be one Christmas these two will remember forever…

Dalton (Book 5)

Dalton Borne is a cowboy who keeps his past closed up inside. He's watched his partners at the New Horizon Ranch find love and he's happy for them and even envious. But his past prevents him from believing he deserves a future that includes a love of his own. But then one stormy night he rescues a very pregnant Rae Anne Tyson from floodwaters and ends up delivering her baby on the side of the road. Suddenly Dalton's life is turned upside down and no matter what he believes he does or doesn't deserve—he can't walk away from helping Rae Anne.

Don't miss book 5 in the New Horizon Ranch series…Dalton Borne is one Texas cowboy you'll never forget.

Sign up for Debra Clopton's Newsletter to find out about future books as soon as they're released!
http://debraclopton.com/contest/

More Books by Debra Clopton

Mule Hollow Matchmakers Series
The Trouble with Lacy Brown (Book 1)
And Baby Makes Five (Book 2)

The Men of Mule Hollow Series
Her Forever Cowboy (Book 1)
Cowboy for Keeps (Book 2)
Yuletide Cowboy (Book 3)

The Cowboys of Sunrise Ranch
Her Unforgettable Cowboy (Book 1)
Her Unexpected Cowboy (Book 2)
Her Unlikely Cowboy (Book 3)

For the complete list, visit her website
www.debraclopton.com

Made in the USA
Charleston, SC
22 December 2016